The Mysterious Mr Marcellus

A SWEET REGENCY NOVELLA

TOMI TABB

Created with Vellum

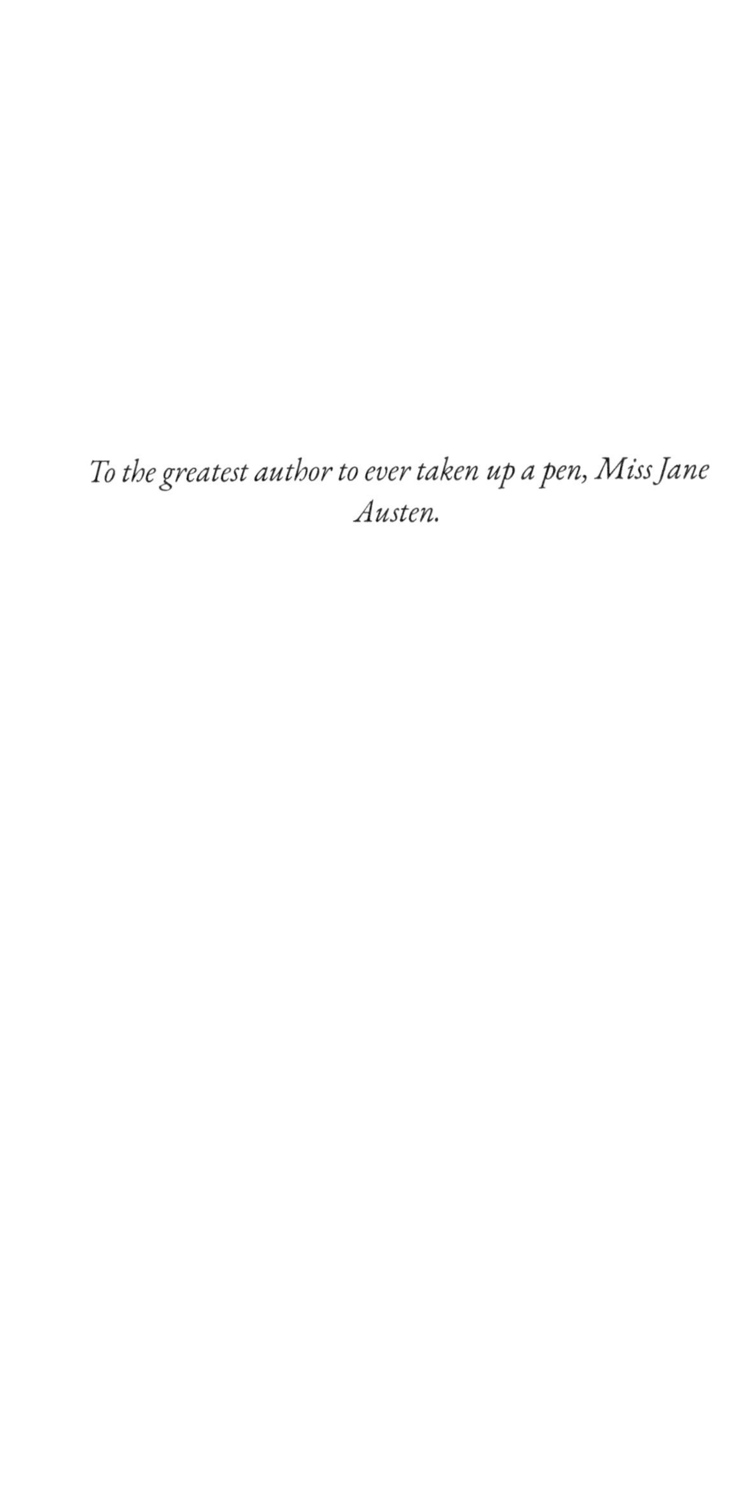

To the greatest author to ever taken up a pen, Miss Jane Austen.

Chapter One

Helen Davenport was keenly aware she ought not to listen in on private conversations. Her governess had always told her as much, but in moments such as these, exceptions could be made. After all, it wasn't everyday one's entire future was at stake.

She pressed her ear against the cold brass keyhole on the door of her father's study. Inside, she could hear the fire crackling. The boots of her would-be suitor, Mr. Thomas Chapman, tread across the squeaky, loose floorboard opposite her father's favorite chair.

In an agitated voice, Mr. Chapman exclaimed, "You, sir, had led me to believe that Miss Davenport's dowry was *much* more substantial than this paltry sum."

Helen heard the sound of shuffling papers. Her heart beat against her ribs as if it were an unruly thoroughbred stallion galloping through a field.

Her father sighed. She could picture him removing his glasses and rubbing his eyes. Calmly, he replied, "As you may be aware, Mr. Chapman, fortune has not smiled kindly upon my estate this past year. Between the flood damage from the River Lea and the poor harvest yield, I've been forced to borrow funds from—"

Mr. Chapman abruptly cut her father off. "I have no care for your excuses, sir. I should have listened to the advice of my friends and steered clear of the country gentry." He stomped towards the door. "I have wasted my time and my efforts in courting a penniless country chit."

Helen covered her mouth with her hand. Her muscles tensed.

Wasted efforts? A penniless country chit? She conjured an image of the afternoon riverside walks she'd taken with Mr. Chapman. He'd been every inch the gentleman these last few weeks.

What happened to the man who read her poetry under the shade of an oak tree? The man who offered to ride into town during a thunderstorm so that she might have the perfect frame for her watercolor painting?

She'd allowed herself to hope it might finally be her turn to marry. Now, her fate as a spinster was all but sealed.

"I'm sorry you feel that way," her father said.

A chair scraped against the floor. She heard Mr. Chapman exhale. Helen immediately inched away from the door and scrambled over to her favorite chaise seat near the front window of the sitting room.

Helen adjusted her skirt and, with shaky, clammy hands, picked up the wooden hoop containing her embroidery sampler. Her needle stabbed the rough cotton.

She was nearly three and twenty. She'd had four unsuccessful Seasons in London and only two offers of courtship. She knew Papa wouldn't be able to afford another Season.

Her father's study door flew open. Without so much as a glance in her direction, Mr. Chapman strode out of the Davenport abode with haste. From the window, she watched as he yanked the reins out of the hands of a waiting groom and bolted onto his horse's saddle.

"Let's go, boy. There is nothing more for us here."

She swallowed hard and watched the bay gelding canter down the narrow lane away from the Winterbrook estate.

"Goodbye, Mr. Chapman," she whispered.

Her cheeks burned in shame, and a stray tear escaped from the corner of her eyes. She swallowed it, letting the taste of bitter salt linger on her tongue. The sampler fell from her hands and clattered onto the floor.

She had promised herself she would not grow upset again if nothing came of Mr. Chapman.

Do not my connections to an earl at least count for something?

Helen felt hopeless and lost. She dabbed her eyes with the sleeve of her dress. At the present, there was nothing else she could do. She breathed deeply.

She supposed they were ill-suited to one another in the first place. Mr. Chapman only cared for entertaining. Like her father, she preferred books to the company of people.

The hinges on her father's study door creaked. Hugh Davenport, a man in his early fifties with greying hair and large amber eyes, stood at the doorway holding his spectacles.

She stood. "Papa?"

He placed his arms behind his back. "And just how much of our conversation did you hear, my dear?"

She bit her lip. "Everything."

His shoulders hunched. He carried himself as if the weight of the world rested upon his shoulders. "I suppose you ought to come through, then."

Helen nodded silently. She followed her father into one of her favorite rooms of their house. She'd spent countless happy hours of her childhood beside the fire, learning to play chess and to read Latin and Greek.

The red velvet curtains were drawn. Rays from the morning sun illuminated the three towering bookshelves bursting to the brim with rare and first-edition books. Mozart, a marmalade-orange cat, was curled up tight on the woven rug in front of the fire, his striped tail shading his eyes from the light.

Papa poured himself a finger of brandy from the crystal decanter on the far side of his cherry desk, which took up the middle of the room. Helen settled herself in the red velvet chair across from the desk.

She watched as her father downed the brandy in one gulp. He gestured to his only child. "No thank you, Papa."

"Just as well," he muttered, gazing longingly out the bay window. Birds chirped cheerfully. "I wish your excellent mother were still alive. She would have the right words of encouragement on hand to soothe your disappointment."

He reached into his pocket and retrieved his watch fob. His large fingers brushed the rim of the miniature portrait he kept of his late wife. "Your mother was gifted in the art of conversation. A natural hostess. Not a recluse like myself. I have done poorly by her."

The sunlight illuminated the sprinkles of silver atop his head. He appeared so much older.

This will not do, Helen thought.

"Papa." She pushed her sadness aside. "It isn't possible to tell what Mama may or may not have done. Mama has been gone for fifteen years." She stood and placed a hand on her father's shoulder. He relaxed under her touch.

"Even when Mama was alive, I was always weary of company. There is no other father in all of England who has done as much for their daughter as you have."

Helen's governess may have taught her to paint, play the pianoforte, speak French, and to dance, but Papa was the one who helped her when she fell off a horse learning to ride. He was right beside her teaching her how to swim in the event she ever fell into the river. He had always ensured she was looked after and, more importantly, ensured that she was loved.

She studied the portrait of the honey, brown-haired woman with blue eyes hanging in the place of honor behind her father's desk. When Helen gazed into a looking glass, her mother's reflection stared back at her as a mirrored image. The only difference was their eyes. Helen's were amber.

The woman who had birthed her was a stranger. Helen wished she could say she recalled her mother's voice, or her laughing, musical nature, but all she had were the cherished stories from her father.

The late Mrs. Davenport had been the eldest child of the Earl of Greenly. In spite of her family's objections, her mother had chosen to marry her father for love. Even all these years later, Papa still mourned her passing. The entirety of his wardrobe consisted of black clothing.

Her father patted her hand. "It is nice of you to say so, but I am well aware of how selfish I have been by keeping you here and to myself most of the year at Winterbrook. 'Tis time we were away to London."

Helen shook her head. "No, Papa. I enjoy our time together." Her stomach muscles clenched. "You and I both know another Season in London is not an option. I've seen the estate ledgers. We cannot afford it."

"That is where you, my dear, are mistaken." He cleared his throat. "I've managed to scrape together just enough funds to give you another Season. Just before Mr. Chapman arrived, a letter came through from your Uncle William and Aunt Sarah. They're expecting us at the end of the month."

Her pulse raced. This was all too good to be true. Could it indeed be possible? Another Season and chance to find a husband?

"But Papa, the estate did not take in any income this year."

"Winterbrook will always provide." The corners of his mouth folded upwards. "I've sold off a portion of the east fields to our neighbors, the Holbrooks. Your ten-thousand-pound dowry is still intact." Her father winked.

"I don't understand." Helen's mouth opened and closed.

I was always told my dowry was five thousand pounds.

"A gift from your Uncle William."

She nodded slowly. The wheels in her mind spun. Something was not adding up. "Papa… if you received a letter from Uncle William this morning knowing full well we were to travel to London and of the added funds to my dowry, why was Mr. Chapman so insulted?"

Nonchalantly, he slid a folded piece of paper to her. Her hand brushed her father's knuckles. "This is what Mr. Chapman was shown."

She opened the crinkled piece paper and read the scribbled sum with pursed lips.

One thousand pounds. It was no wonder Mr. Chapman left in the manner that he did.

"I may have forgotten to add an additional zero to the sum. In my old age, I'm becoming a rather forgetful old man." Papa sat behind his desk, his cheeks flushed a rosy red.

"In truth, I never approved of Mr. Chapman. He lacked your wit and intelligence. When he began to question whether or not you were to inherit the estate, I had my suspicions, and so I decided to test Mr. Chapman. I would never accept a man who would seek to marry *my* daughter solely for material gain."

"I no longer harbor any grand illusions, Papa." Helen sank into the chair across from him. "If I shall be lucky enough in life to find a husband who may provide me with a comfortable home, a roof over my head, and a child, I shall be content."

"I wish you would not give up on love so easily. You must have more faith." Papa sighed. "Love works in mysterious ways, my dear."

She bit her lip to keep herself from speaking out. In this, her father's mind would not be changed. Helen vividly remembered the night her father had escorted her to her first London ball. Inside the carriage, he had expressed a desire for her to make a love match even if it meant waiting an entire lifetime.

She'd dreamed of finding a man just like her father. But as the Seasons passed, Helen had come to learn that unfortunately, that man did not exist. At this point in her life, so long as her potential future husband allowed her to read what she wished, she would be happy. Odysseus would always be a welcomed friend over any of the latest gothic novels.

Helen thought back to each of her last four London Seasons. All of them had ended without a proposal in sight.

This time will be different. I will not waste the opportunity Papa has put before me. I can't let him down again. This Season will be different.

Chapter Two

Three weeks later, a footman handed Helen down from the Davenport carriage. Her legs wobbled, unsteady and stiff from sitting for three hours. Moving her feet brought the blood back to her limbs, easing the ache.

She studied the identical white bricked townhouses lining the street. Tightly packed together, the only distinguishing feature of the homes was the numbers on the front of each door.

Adjusting her bonnet, she followed her father up the front entry steps of her aunt and uncle's home. Papa rapped on the black door to number twelve Curzon Street.

A moment later, it swung open. "Hello, Watson, is your master at home?" her father asked.

As Watson opened his mouth to reply, a deep male voice bellowed from the drawing room, "Hugh, about time you arrived."

Papa tilted his head to the side. "Ever the impatient man, William is."

The wizened butler remained stone faced as he showed them inside. "I shall see to the unpacking of your luggage." He bowed to them. "Mr. Davenport, Miss Davenport welcome to London."

"Thank you, Watson."

They showed themselves into the familiar circular room adorned in scarlet-and-brown-toned wallpaper. The room had not changed in more than five years.

A portly man dressed in cream-colored wool breeches, a blue waistcoat, a white cravat, and an olive tailcoat stood from his seat on the scarlet chaise lounge. "Aren't you a sight for sore eyes, Davenport? You've grown old, man."

"William, you're one to speak," Papa retorted. "I prefer to view the process of aging as becoming more distinguished with time, like a fine vintage wine." Lord William Rankin, the Earl of Greenly, clapped her father on the back.

"Ah, there is my lovely niece. Let me have a look at you." Uncle William signaled for Helen to come closer.

She hastily removed her bonnet, smoothed her hair, and curtsied. "Uncle William."

"None of this. Formalities don't exist in the Rankin household," he laughed.

Helen straightened herself and hugged him tightly, breathing in the scent of whisky and tobacco smoke.

"You, my sweet girl, have grown even more beautiful than the last time I laid eyes on you. I dare say I shall have to direct Watson to restrict the number of callers you're likely to receive over the coming weeks."

Helen's cheeks burned. Uncle William's words flattered her. Rarely was she ever referred to as attractive. Those words were reserved normally for the young debutantes who came from families of wealth and could afford the highest-quality clothing, jewelry, and French maids to style their hair.

"She takes after her mother," Papa said in a muted tone. "A rare and classic beauty."

"Of course she does," Aunt Sarah replied, entering the room.

Lady Sarah Rankin was a woman of short stature with blonde hair and emerald-green eyes. What she lacked in height, she made up for with a personality as large as that of her husband. In her early forties, she had birthed two sons, both of whom had married, with families of their own. From the gleam in her eye, Helen had little doubt of Aunt Sarah's plans for herself.

"Aunt Sarah." Helen hugged her tightly.

"Let me have a look at you." Helen spun in a circle.

"Time has passed too quickly. You are a woman grown," Aunt Sarah lamented.

Her father and Uncle William stepped over to the nearest bookshelf, examining a few of the latest purchases from Hatchards, a famed bookseller located in Piccadilly Circus.

"Not here five minutes and William already has your father engrossed in a book," Sarah chided, shaking her head. "At least when we are out shopping tomorrow, I shan't feel any trace of guilt in leaving them to fend for themselves."

"We're going shopping?" Helen tilted her head to the side. "I had several new day dresses and a ballgown made up for myself before Papa and I left Winterbrook."

"That is all well and good, but what of your gloves, hat, shoes, stockings, and your undergarments?"

Heat rushed through her body. "What I have is serviceable." She rubbed the nape of her neck.

Aunt Sarah raised an eyebrow. "You are no longer in the country, dearest. Serviceable will not do you any favors amongst the Ton. You are under *my* care now." She placed her hands on Helen's shoulders. The weight of them was comforting.

"Shopping is about more than picking out new trinkets. Whilst we are out tomorrow, you'll be introduced to several key acquaintances of myself and Lord Greenly. Their support will go far in securing invitations to the most sought-after engagements, such as Lady Woodrow's ball, over the next few weeks."

She had never thought about how shopping could be like a game of chess. It was all about tactics. She blinked slowly. "Thank you, Aunt Sarah. I don't know what I might do without you."

"I only wish your father had enlisted our assistance when you first made your debut." Aunt Sarah sighed. "Nevertheless, you're here now, and rest assured, I'm going to do everything in my power to find you the *right* husband."

Helen resisted the urge to wince. Aunt Sarah was so confident. How could she be so certain of Helen's success? Each of the last four Seasons, it was difficult to earn any invitations. The women of the highest echelons of society, the first circle, would instantly see that she had little to offer their sons. Her dowry was small and she had so few connections.

Aunt Sarah redirected her attention to Papa, her eyes narrowed. "It is high time Hugh's clothing was also addressed," she whispered into Helen's ear. "Your mother would never have wished him to mourn her for so long. We'll send a message to Lord Greenly's tailor in the morning. Best we launch a surprise attack."

"Just like the ancient Greeks at the Battle of Marathon," Helen said.

"Indeed. Who knows, perhaps with a change of wardrobe, your father might even consider finding himself another wife. If he has a companion, it might help to make the transition easier when you began your married life and say farewell to Winterbrook."

Helen froze.

Leave Papa and Winterbrook? They had both been a constant in her life. Since she was a girl, Papa has always been right by her side.

She watched her father engage Uncle William in a debate over the context and meaning of a word translated from a Latin treatise of Cicero.

If I am gone, who will take care of him? Who will see to the tenants? I've been so focused on myself that I've lost sight of how marriage would affect those around me.

Helen lowered her head. A thin layer of dust coated her pelisse.

Understanding her niece's plight, Aunt Sarah said in

a raised voice, "You both must be fatigued from all of the traveling. Would you care to refresh yourselves?" The men didn't stir. Aunt Sarah pressed her lips together.

Over the years, Helen had learned if she wanted her father's attention when he was occupied by a new book, she had to physically attain it. Walking over to her father, she tapped him on the shoulder.

In a matter-of-fact tone, trying to imitate Aunt Sarah, she said, "Papa, we must change."

Her father blinked slowly several times. "Change?"

"Yes, Papa. We are coated in dust from the road."

"I had you placed on the second floor in your normal rooms," Aunt Sarah added quickly. "I'll have Watson send up your valet and maid."

"Quite right." Papa snapped the heavily bound volume he was reading closed and placed it back upon Uncle William's bookshelf. "We'll continue our debate after the evening meal."

Aunt Sarah winked.

Helen squared her shoulders and stood tall. Perhaps being confident was easier than she had thought.

Excusing themselves, she and her father exited the room.

The fog had lifted. The morning sun emerged from behind the patchwork of remaining storm clouds. Puddles of water dotted the walkway. Helen was mindful of her steps as she walked out the next morning.

The trees and floral displays of Hyde Park provided

an oasis of escape from the urban sprawl of London. Birds chirped out, busy at work feeding their young. The air was fresh with a slight scent of wet dirt.

"I have a favorite spot on the knoll across from the Serpentine, where the swans often linger. It's a bit of a walk," Helen said to her footman as he carried the basket containing her blanket, sketchbook, and pencils.

The young footman kept his facial expression neutral. "Very good, Miss Davenport."

She glanced over her shoulder.

This will not do.

"Please don't feel obliged to walk behind me. If you speak with any member of the senior staff, you'll find my father and I are quite like Lord and Lady Greenly—eccentric and at times unconventional. We wish for our servants to be seen, not to be invisible."

She was rewarded with an upturn of the corners of his mouth.

Helen continued. "If we are to spend the morning in one another's company, it's only fair, I have your name."

"I'm John, miss."

"John. That's an amiable name." She placed her hands behind her back.

He must be a newer servant. She didn't remember him from the last time she and Papa stayed at Curzon Street.

"Have you worked in service long?"

"I've worked in Lord and Lady Greenly's household for just over one year. My brother is also a footman."

Helen wracked her brain, reviewing the names and faces of the servants who had always been kind to her, and remembered one with curly brown hair similar to John's. She snapped her fingers together. "Samuel."

John raised his eyebrows. "That's him, miss."

Around them, the morning breeze caused the surrounding tree branches to sway and creak. They talked more as they walked deeper into the park.

She learned John had four other younger siblings who resided with his parents in Kent. He was sixteen years of age and aspired one day to rise to become a gentleman's valet or, if fortune smiled upon him, a butler.

They slowed their pace, and Helen soaked in the majestic sight of the sun reflecting off the edge of the Serpentine, the sky awash in pink and orange hues. A family of five adult swans lay clustered together on the sandy banks of the pond with their heads tucked under their wings, fast asleep.

This is exactly the scene I hoped to capture, Helen thought. *Now the question is, where shall I sit and sketch?*

She surveyed the area. Her gaze turned to the knoll of grass directly across from the Serpentine. Walking over to it, she bent her knees and removed the leather glove from her right hand. The ground was damp, but firm.

She gestured to the basket John was holding. "If you would be so kind as to please unpack the blanket that I asked Watson to include in our supply kit, we'll establish ourselves here."

John nodded and set to work unpacking the thick, heavy item just as a large gust of wind caused the now-lighter picnic basket to blow over. Helen's sketchpad and pencils fell out, rolling down the hill and onto the dirt path. She rushed over to retrieve them.

In the distance, she heard the telltale clip-clop of horse hooves galloping against the path. A muffled male voice yelled out. Helen strained her neck, searching for the direction the horse was coming from. Her pulse quickened.

"Miss Davenport!" John exclaimed.

As she glanced over her shoulder, a massive black stallion galloped towards her. Her mind urged her to move, yet her body froze. Instinctively, she knew she wouldn't be able to jump out of its path in time. Her arms moved to cover her head and neck, and she braced for impact.

Chapter Three

The impact, however, never came. Instead, Helen felt John's strong hands grab hold of her body. With two hearts frantically beating as one, he dove with Helen cradled to his chest. For several terrifying moments, the world blurred as they both rolled. She squeezed her eyes shut. Sounds were muffled. Rocks scratched against the tender flesh of her bare arms. Mud entered her mouth.

Then, in an instant, it was over. She breathed sharply in short gasps. Opening her eyes, black dots danced in her field of vision, yet otherwise, she felt no pain. Slowly, she sat up. From her position, she could discern John's form lay sprawled out to her immediate left. His chest rose and fell sharply.

He had saved her life.

"John," she croaked.

His head turned in her direction. The corners of his eyes crinkled in pain.

"You… a'right… miss?" he wheezed out.

"Fine." She spit out the frozen mud. "And yourself?"

"Brilliant," John asserted stubbornly.

With all the strength she could muster, she rushed over to his side. His royal-blue coat was covered in mud. He breathed shallowly, clenching his jaw. It was then that she noticed the unnatural angle of his arm. Her stomach lurched.

You have to be as strong as your namesake, Helen of Troy. John needs you.

"John, why didn't you say your arm was injured?" she asked softly.

"Nothing you can do about it," he whimpered.

She brushed a lock of his hair away from his face. His cheeks were warm to the touch as he huffed in pain, concerning her. "I will do everything in my power to see you recovered. I owe you my life."

Through sheer force of will, Helen kept herself from panicking. Adrenaline coursed through her body.

They were in Hyde Park alone, and John's arm was broken.

Her eyes swept the periphery. The knoll was deserted. Most of London slept, preferring to keep later, more fashionable Town hours.

She was going to have to leave John alone to find help, but she didn't want to abandon him in such a state.

Helen could vaguely recall reading one of her papa's medical books. For once in her life, being a bluestocking might be advantageous. She chanced a second glance to his arm and quickly looked away.

A sweat had broken over John's brow, and his arm had to be stabilized to keep from further damaging it.

What materials did she have at her disposal? Paper, pencils, and a blanket. All of those items were useless.

The awakening swans fluttered their wings. A curious adult swan approached them, poking its beak at the muddied hem of her petticoat. He honked, disappointed the clothing item wasn't food.

"The petticoat! Eureka," Helen whispered.

Without a care for who might see her, she pulled her knees to her chest and placed the edge of the petticoat in her mouth. The thin cotton fabric tore with ease into a long strip.

The sound of running steps approached them. Helen stayed focused on the task at hand. A man kneeled down, panting. He smelled of sandalwood. Out of the corner of her eye, she could see the man shrugging off his greatcoat and tailcoat.

"What has happened?" The man spoke with an air of authority.

"Runaway horse. Miss Davenport needs help," John muttered.

Helen dropped the fabric from her mouth. She shook her head. "I am fine. John is the one who's been injured."

She could feel the heavy fabric of a man's greatcoat being draped around her shoulders, protecting her from the morning chill. The man's gaze met Helen's. His brown hair was wild and stuck out in a variety of angles. His cheeks were colored a shade of bright cherry red.

Deep turquoise eyes bored into her with concern. "How may I be of assistance?"

"Dip this in the Serpentine. The cool water will hopefully cool his flushed skin."

The man nodded. Taking the fabric from her hands, he sprinted over to the river and returned momentarily. He passed her the dampened cloth.

Helen set to work in patting down John's neck and forehead. The man released the diamond stick pin from his cravat and began to untie it. Helen raised an eyebrow.

"To bind his arm," he stated matter-of-factly.

John's eyes fluttered. "I am sorry to be a burden, miss."

"Do not dare consider yourself a burden," Helen said in a muted tone. "You are a hero, like the mighty Achilles."

"Have you heard the tale of Achilles, lad?" the stranger asked.

John replied that he had not.

"Perhaps we can implore the lady to tell you more about him."

He thinks quickly on his feet.

"Achilles was said to be the greatest hero in all of the ancient world. He was a prince, a warrior, and a demi-god." Helen moved over to John's side and continued to cool his body. "Throughout the ten years the Trojan War was fought, there was not a single warrior who could defeat Achilles unless they hit the one part of his body that was vulnerable—his heel."

"That's an odd body part to leave unprotected," John wheezed.

"I fully agree with you, but consider this: When Achilles was but a child, he was dipped upside down by his mother into the Underworld's River Styx. His parents hoped that it would prevent a prophecy that declared Achilles would die in battle. But little did they know, the one area that was left exposed was the area where his mother had held him."

"Funny things, prophecies. It was the measures people took to prevent them that often resulted in them coming true." The stranger's forehead creased. "I point to the tales of Oedipus and Antigone as proof."

"I agree with you, sir," Helen said.

The gentleman knows his Greek myths and legends well.

John's eyebrows furrowed. "I don't understand."

Helen had momentarily forgotten about her young charge. "Our friend means that it was fate. Humans could not control their destiny, as much as they might have wished."

The man cleared his throat. His eyes were creased and mouth tight. "Lad, we must have you seen by a physician straightaway. However, I won't lie. Your arm is in a state and it must be stabilized before we can move you. I will do my best not to jostle the limb any more than necessary."

John grunted. "Do it."

"Squeeze this if it hurts." Helen moved to his side and offered him her hand.

Making eye contact with her, the man said, "I will work as quickly as I dare." He gazed to John. "Lad, are you ready?"

John blew out a long breath. "Yes, sir."

True to his word, the man gently lifted him and slipped the knotted cravat around the appendage. Helen chewed her lip. John sucked in air, but kept his cries to himself and squeezed Helen's hand, hard. It felt as if it were locked in a vice. Perspiration and tears poured down his cheeks.

"It's done." The man ran a hand through John's tussled hair. "Well done, lad. You are braver than Achilles, you are a young Hercules. The Greeks may have appreciated their heroes, but the Romans worshiped them."

"Thank you," Helen said, letting out a deep breath. John's hand still held hers.

The man inclined his head. "I would be remiss in my duties as a gentleman if I didn't see to those in need."

"The horse came upon us so quickly. I was unaware of what was happening until John pulled me down."

"Indeed." The man frowned. "My horse and I were attempting to catch that spooked, riderless mount when we happened upon you."

She shivered. The damp from the ground had soaked into her clothing. She pulled the heavy fabric of the jacket in tighter, beginning to feel a dull ache all over her body.

"We must get you two out of the cold." The gentleman glanced uncertainly in John's direction.

"Sir, if you would kindly ride to number twelve Curzon Street, you will find the residence of Lord Greenly, where my father and I are guests. They'll send us help and the carriage."

"Will you both be all right on your own?"

Helen assured him they would.

The man stood and brushed off his breeches. For the first time, she was able to see the high quality and impeccable cut of the clothing. Her cheeks flushed.

She'd also never seen a man so informally attired. Even her own father rarely removed his coat in her presence. Without his cravat, she could make out a set of powerfully sculpted muscles in his chest. She turned her head.

"I shall be as quick as I can." The man placed his fingers into his lips and let out a low whistle. As he slipped on his tailcoat, Helen started to shrug off his greatcoat.

"Please, keep it in your possession."

"But what of you?" Helen's hands fingered the top button of the coat.

"I was raised in the north of England. We're a hearty stock."

A chestnut-colored thoroughbred trotted over to where the trio of them were gathered. The horse nickered at the man's shoulder. He absentmindedly rubbed its muzzle and gripped the reins in his hands. In a single, fluid motion, the man slipped into his saddle. Tipping an invisible hat to her, he spurred his mount into a gallop.

She watched him ride off.

I didn't even think to ask the gentleman his name. I suppose for now, I shall name him Apollo, after the Greek god of light, prophecy, and healing.

To John, she said, "Hold on just a little bit longer. Help is on its way." She patted his hand.

"Very good, Miss Davenport."

The remainder of the morning passed in a blur. The Davenport carriage rolled swiftly into Hyde Park and removed them to Curzon Street. John was whisked from her care and settled in one of the bedrooms on the second floor in spite of his protests. Helen was carried to her room and given a hot bath.

The water was a boon to her aching body. "Miss Davenport, look at the sight of you. I'll search for some cream to sort out the bruising this afternoon," said Patsy, her personal maid.

Helen rolled her neck from side to side. "That would be lovely."

"Your poor father is pacing the hallway, a nervous wreck. His mind won't be put at ease until he sees you are safe and sound."

Patsy assisted her out of the tub. Water dripped from her hair, leaving a small trail as they walked towards the changing screen. Even with the roaring fire in the next room, the temperature was chilly.

"Poor Papa. Was he in a state when the news arrived?"

Patsy handed her a clean night shift. "Watson sent Samuel round to find him. He was en route to the bookseller's shop. I hope never to see him in such a state again."

Helen grimaced at the image of her father's chalk-white, nearly translucent face and haunted eyes. It was the same expression she had seen the day her mother passed on. In all the years, she'd never forgotten it.

They made their way to the dressing room. Helen stared at her reflection, sitting down in front of the vanity mirror. Her eyes were bloodshot and face pale. She pinched her cheeks. "Has there been any word on John?"

"Not that I'm privy to, Miss Davenport." Patsy's practiced hands set to work combing and plaiting her hair in a gentle manner. "You should direct your inquiries to your father."

Helen sighed. "I will."

Patsy tightened the ribbon at the end of her plait. "There."

Helen settled herself into the bed. Her maid tidied up the vanity table and walked towards the door. "Will there be anything else, Miss Davenport?"

Helen had almost forgotten. "This may not be the best of times to mention this, but Mrs. Thorngren will be leaving Winterbrook at the end of the year. Father and I spoke of it this morning and we would like you to consider becoming our next housekeeper."

Patsy's mouth opened and closed. She splayed her hand on her chest. "I would be honored, miss."

"Excellent. Father hoped you might be open to the idea and has already written to Mrs. Thorngren."

Patsy wiped a stray tear from the corner of her eye. "I am ever so lucky to have you and Mr. Davenport as a mistress and master."

"I will miss you dearly, but this is a post you've earned from your years of dedicated service." Helen tightly smiled. "Please send Father in. I am ready." She slid into the covers and pulled them over her legs, sitting up straight against the pillows.

"Helen!" Papa wasted no time in rapidly entered the room, nearly knocking into Patsy. "Child, let me look you over." Her father's face was an ashen grey, his cravat askew and waistcoat buttoned crookedly.

"Papa, aside from being a little sore, I am fully fit," she emphasized.

"We'll see what the physician declares. He'll be here as soon as he's finished with John." Papa placed a kiss atop her head.

Helen sat up straighter in the bed. "How is he?"

"Greenly reports that the physician has set his arm. The break was clean and there is an excellent chance of his regaining its full use."

She breathed a sigh of relief. "Thank goodness. Perhaps I may cross the hall and look in on—"

"You will do no such thing." Papa placed a hand on her shoulder to stop her from leaving the bed. "Let nature take its course. Sleep is the best medicine for the young man."

"But Papa…" Helen protested.

"Nothing you say will sway my mind. You may see him on the morrow." He pulled the covers up around her body and tucked her into the bed in the manner he had when she was younger. "Until the physician assesses you, in bed you will remain."

She sighed. There would be no changing his mind. "Yes, Papa."

Her father settled himself into the chair across from her. "You and I, however, may pass the time discussing Herodotus and *The Histories*."

Helen blinked slowly. "May we at least discuss it in Greek?"

"As you wish."

Helen's mind wandered, reliving the events of the morning in her mind. She could still hear the sound of the approaching horse, smell the mud, and feel John pulling her out of danger's pathway. Her father's calming voice relaxed her frazzled nerves.

"Papa?" Her father stopped reading. He placed his finger on the page as a bookmark and glanced up at her. "The gentleman who brought the news of the accident... did you happen to catch his name?"

Her father removed his glasses from the bridge of his nose. "Unfortunately, not. In the chaos of the moment, Watson was only able to ascertain your young man referred to himself as Marcellus. He left directly to fetch his personal physician and indicated he would call in the next few days."

"Marcellus," she said softly. "What a curious name."

There was a knock at the door. Her father rose from his seat to grant the physician entry. Papa stood off to the side as the physician examined her. Helen was granted a clean bill of health, but to her dismay, was ordered to stay in bed for the next three days.

Three days is entirely too long. One shall be sufficient. A half if I can speak to Aunt Sarah about letting me come below stairs.

They thanked the physician and he departed. Her

father carried himself with a more erect posture. He sat down and picked up the book, continuing to read until Helen's eyes grew heavy and her breathing evened out. She fully surrendered to the realm of Morpheus and the land of dreams.

Chapter Four

It was two days before Helen was granted leave from her bedchamber. She was presently reading in the drawing room while Aunt Sarah sat at her desk composing a return letter to her eldest son. The only sound that filled the room was the scratching of her quill pen. Helen gave up on her well-worn copy of *The Iliad* and snapped it closed.

Aunt Sarah spoke without looking up. "If you are bored, dear, there is a magazine you may glance through to my left. I've earmarked the page with the gown that would suit your coloring well."

A knock sounded on the door. "Enter," Aunt Sarah called out.

Watson entered the room. "My lady, there is a caller here inquiring on the availability of Mr. John and Miss Davenport."

Aunt Sarah placed her pen down and blew on the paper, waiting for the ink to dry.

"Strange, I had thought William asked for the knocker to be removed."

"Apologies, Lady Greenly, but the knocker is not out. This particular caller, however, I thought you may wish to make an exception for."

Helen's heart pounded against her rib cage. She resisted the urge to run to the window and look out onto the front step. Was this the mysterious Marcellus?

Aunt Sarah folded her hands on her lap and raised an eyebrow. "If you believe we should make an exception, Watson, then that is a solid enough reason for me. Does our caller have a card?"

"No, your ladyship. I understand this call was an impromptu decision. The gentleman has given his name as Mr. Marcellus." Watson's lips twitched. It was the closest the longtime butler would come to smiling.

"Please show him in, and please direct the kitchen to send up a pot of tea and some biscuits." Aunt Sarah closed her desk and stood.

Helen's hands shook. She hid them behind her back as their gentleman caller entered the room. Her breath hitched. Mr. Marcellus was even more handsome than she remembered, clad in a suit of light blue with gold trim and highly polished knee-high boots. In this lighting, his brown hair was more of a chocolate color than an ash brown. At his full height, he stood six feet tall, dwarfing her five-foot-three frame.

Removing his hat and gloves, he bowed.

"Mr. Marcellus…" Her aunt hesitated "It is an honor to have you in my home. I am Lady Greenly. Please allow me to introduce you to my goddaughter, Miss Helen Davenport." Helen and her aunt curtsied.

A footman entered the room with a tea service and placed it upon the table between the sofa and the window overlooking the street.

Mr. Marcellus ran a hand through his hair. "Thank you for granting me an audience today, Lady Greenly. You present a lovely home."

"On behalf of my family and my staff, you must allow me to express the utmost gratitude for the service you rendered to my goddaughter and footman. We will forever be indebted to you."

Aunt Sarah gestured for them to sit.

"I was only doing what any worthy gentleman would do." He crossed his long legs and drummed his fingers against the arms of the chaise. "Miss Davenport, I am thrilled to see you well. Are you fully recovered?"

Helen placed her hands on her lap and clasped them tightly together. "As you can see, Mr. Marcellus, I am indeed restored to full health."

Her body grew warm. Just a few days ago, she hadn't any difficulty in conversing with their guest, and now, Helen's mind drew a blank. What else should she say to him?

Aunt Sarah inclined her head towards the tea. Helen stood and set to work at preparing three cups, grateful for the distraction.

"And Master John? How is he faring?"

"John is recovering well. Now that the worst of the pain has passed, his appetite has returned with a vengeance." Aunt Sarah chuckled.

"Excellent." Mr. Marcellus sat up straighter.

"Our John will be disappointed that he has missed your visit. If you would be so inclined, would you consider looking in on him before you depart?" her aunt asked.

Mr. Marcellus nodded. "Indeed, I shall."

Helen placed two sugars into a cup for her aunt. Steam billowed above the teapot, creating swirling patterns in the air around them. This blend's scent was spicy, with hints of lemon.

"Mr. Marcellus, how do you take your tea?" she asked.

"Straight, if you would be so kind."

Wordlessly, she poured a cup and placed a ginger biscuit on the saucer. As she passed the cup to Mr. Marcellus, their gazes met. The deep pools of aquamarine were a lighter shade than the morning of the accident, nearly stormlike and full of uncertainty.

"I thank you." With shaky hands, he took a sip of the tea. "Miss Davenport, may I ask, the copy of *The Iliad* on the chaise sofa… does that belong to you? It is not a book which ladies often choose to read."

Helen's pulse began to race. How should she answer such the question? Would Mr. Marcellus be the type of man who immediately dismissed her for her unorthodox education?

I only have one chance to form a favorable impression.

Her gaze traveled to her aunt for direction. Closing her eyes, Aunt Sarah took hold of her cup of tea and subtly nodded.

"Yes, Mr. Marcellus, the book was a gift from my

father for my tenth name day. I have been…" She hesitated "Inspired by recent events to revisit the story of Helen of Troy, Paris, Menelaus, and Agamemnon."

Mr. Marcellus appraised her. "You cannot forget the mighty Achilles."

Butterflies fluttered in her stomach. "My mistake."

He picked up the copy of the book and turned it over in his hands. The binding was loose, some of the corner of the pages folded over. Her cheeks grew warm. If he did not think her a bluestocking before, he certainly would now when he noticed the book was in Greek.

"Do you have a favorite book, sir?" She folded her hands on her lap.

Mr. Marcellus's gaze traveled up to her face. "I enjoy reading a wide array of works, though I have a particular fondness for Cicero and Marcus Aurelius."

Aunt Sarah chuckled. "A pity my husband and Mr. Davenport are not present. They'd thoroughly enjoy making your acquaintance."

He tilted his head to the side.

"My father and my uncle are always keen to meet another person who shares their enjoyment of the classics," Helen said.

Aunt Sarah placed her nearly empty teacup on the table. *Goodness me! Where has the time gone?*

As much as Helen may have wished for Mr. Marcellus to stay longer, she was reminded that she was no longer at Winterbrook, where she was the mistress of the house. Number twelve Curzon Street was the home of her aunt.

There were some unspoken rules that even Aunt

Sarah would never break, and a morning call longer than fifteen minutes was one of them.

Mr. Marcellus stood, clutching the rim of his hat tightly. "I thank you for your hospitality this morning. May I inquire if I may call upon you ladies in two days' time? Perhaps Mr. Davenport and your husband will be available?"

The ladies stood. "We would welcome renewing our acquaintance with you. As for my husband, I cannot speak for him, but I will be certain to pass your request to him."

"Excellent." He straightened his cravat. "Then if you would please have a servant direct me to Master John's room, I'll visit with the lad before I depart."

Just as Helen was about to offer her service to Mr. Marcellus, her aunt pulled the red cord to request a footman.

Aunt Sarah shot her a tight smile.

The door opened. "Lady Greenly?" a footman asked.

"Ah, Samuel. Please lead our guest up to John's room."

"Certainly, my lady."

He bowed once more before departing. With a heavy thud, the drawing room's doors were closed.

"Aunt, why could I not have taken Mr. Marcellus up to John's room?" Helen sank into her seat on the chaise, her hands absently running over the cover of *The Iliad*.

"Polite society follows strict rules about how to call upon and receive a guest. Mr. Marcellus may appear to be a gentleman, but I have some reservations."

Helen couldn't understand her aunt. "What reservations could you possibly hold against the man? Did he not prove himself based upon his actions in Hyde Park?" she sputtered.

"His actions from a few days ago is the reason why I agreed to our seeing the man." Aunt Sarah sighed. "We have only *just* become formally acquainted with him. We know very little of his character or his connections. Your uncle has made discrete inquiries, yet he could not find a single person who knew of a person named Mr. Marcellus. It is as if he materialized out of thin air, my dear."

Helen pinched the bridge of her nose. "I know you mean well, Aunt, and that you are trying to protect me from the likes of men like Mr. Chapman."

"Take heart, sweetling. I happen to find Mr. Marcellus very agreeable." Aunt Sarah picked up her teacup.

Helen locked eyes with her. "You do?"

"Certainly. Just because I wish to approach this connection cautiously does not mean I do not approve of the chap. We'll just have to wait and see how our next visit unfolds."

Are you playing the matchmaking game, Aunt Sarah? Should I be fearful?

As Helen adjusted her position on the chaise, she felt a sharp pinch on her hip. Glancing to her right, she noticed a parcel wrapped in a thin layer of twine. Her heart skipped a few beats. In elegant black script, the top of the package read: "For the Nymph of Hyde Park."

Quickly, she covered the item with her book. "Aunt, do you mind if I return this to my room?"

The entry hall door opened and closed. From the

window, she watched as the lanky silhouette of Mr. Marcellus disappeared down the steps and across the road towards Hyde Park.

"By all means, dearest."

Inside her room, Helen firmly closed the door. Sitting at her dressing table with shaking hands, she inspected the parcel closer.

It was from the book shop, Hatchards. Did Mr. Marcellus mean to leave it for her? Or did it fall from his pocket?

With a pull, she unknotted the twine and ripped apart the brown paper. Inside was an English-language copy of *The Iliad*. The cover was made from red leather with gold lettering. As she opened it, she soaked in the hand-painted images of scenes from the book. It was a collector's quality book. She was afraid to know how much it cost.

She clutched it to her chest. She could smell the scent of the glue holding the book together. Even if Mr. Marcellus did not intend to gift her the book, she was keeping it. This was a treasure.

Against all odds, for the first time in her four Seasons, Helen found herself pining for a man she knew virtually nothing about. Her stomach fluttered full of butterflies. Her cheeks grew warm thinking about the fine figure he cut on a horse. Two days could not pass quickly enough.

Chapter Five

"We must have visited every establishment on Bond Street," Helen mused as they entered her aunt's preferred millinery shop to the jingle of a bell.

Shelves from floor to ceiling displayed bonnets trimmed with colorful ribbons, turbans, and other accessories a lady might wish to use as hair ornaments. Helen's gloved hand traced the tip of an orange feather. Its fringed edges danced under her touch.

The shop's owner was assisting a mother and daughter. Aunt Sarah glanced over a paper list as they waited. "This is to be our final shop before we stop for a spot of tea. After which, we'll visit the boot and glove makers."

Helen nodded. She'd long given up attempting to protest the sheer amount of shopping Aunt Sarah had planned.

How could her aunt's ideas differ so drastically from what Helen deemed to be serviceable? Should clothing not be purchased more for comfort than appearances?

She understood having one or two fine ball gowns made up, but five or six day dresses too?She'd much rather spend the funds on paper, ink, or a good book. Fashion changed too suddenly to be able to keep up with the latest trends.

Aunt Sarah returned the list to her reticule.

The mother and daughter turned. "Lady Greenly, what a marvelous surprise."

The woman was dressed in a frock cut from a fine maroon brocade, her daughter in a cream dress. Both women had similar features of curly blonde locks and blue eyes.

"Lady Woodrow, Miss Alice. How lovely to see you both." Aunt Sarah inclined her head. "May I introduce you to my niece and goddaughter, Miss Helen Davenport of Winterbrook in Hertfordshire." Helen curtsied.

"Miss Davenport. How are you finding your stay in London to be so far? Has the excitement of the Season caught up with you yet?" Lady Woodrow inquired.

"I am enjoying my stay very much. There are so many more amusements in London to enjoy than in the country." Helen crossed her fingers behind her back.

"Indeed, I couldn't agree more." Lady Woodrow slipped a pair of gloves over her hands. "You two ladies simply must call on us for tea later this week. Oh, and we must have you attend our ball! I'll sent a footman over with an invitation later today."

A two-minute conversation, and just like that, Helen's aunt had secured an invitation to one of the most exclusive events to open the Season.

Aunt Sarah and Lady Woodrow exchanged a few

more words, then parted ways. The shop's owner patiently lingered in the background.

Like a colonel commanding his troops, Aunt Sarah wasted no time and efficiently placed an order for two bonnets and two feathered hair pieces.

Outside once more, Helen could sense a change in her aunt's mood. Her body was rigid with tension, her jaw clenched. "Helen, we must return home straightaway."

"Aunt?" She placed her hand on her aunt's forearm.

"Lady Woodrow has a keen ear for gossip. There are few rumors or happenings that occur in town without her becoming privy to it." Aunt Sarah glanced nervously around them. Ladies and gentlemen strolled leisurely up and down the street, enjoying one of the few spells of dry weather over the past day.

Lowering her voice, her aunt said, "Word is spreading of an incident that took place in Hyde Park involving a young lady and a gentleman in a shocking state of undress."

Helen's breathing quickened. Was the story referring to the accident? How could this be? She wracked her brain. She couldn't remember seeing any other people nearby.

"There is a perfectly logical explanation for what happened. Could we not merely explain the runaway horse and the near collision?" she whispered.

"The Ton lives for vile gossip." Aunt Sarah took hold of Helen's hands. "If there is even a whisper that you are connected to the incident, the gossip will take on a life of its own and your reputation, my dear, will be ruined."

"Ruined?" Helen grew light-headed. "But all that a woman has in life is her reputation." Her heart thumped against her ribs.

"It will not come to that, my dear. We'll discuss how we are to address the gossip in private once we arrive home."

"I hope you are right, Aunt."

Signaling their carriage, Aunt Sarah and Helen alighted and sped off to Curzon Street.

The moment they entered the hallway, Watson informed the ladies that Mr. Marcellus had been waiting for them to return.

Helen's chest grew tight. He wasn't supposed to call until tomorrow. Why had he opted to call upon them today?

She and Aunt Sarah quickly removed their hats and outerwear, placing it in Watson's outstretched arms.

Do I have time to have Patsy adjust my hair? Should I pinch my cheeks for some added color?

"Please see to a pot of tea and plate of refreshments—"

Watson cleared his throat. "It has all been taken care of, Lady Greenly."

"Thank you, Watson." Aunt Sarah breathed a sigh of relief. Watson nodded curtly and excused himself. "After twenty years, the man still manages to surprise me with how efficient he is."

Helen placed a hand on her stomach and reminded herself to breathe. She nodded to her aunt.

A footman opened the door. Mr. Marcellus stood with his hands placed behind his back, staring out the window. He looked to be lost in his thoughts. She admired his strong jawline and broad chest.

"Mr. Marcellus." Aunt Sarah entered the room ahead of Helen. "I apologize no one was in to receive you until now."

"Lady Greenly. Miss Davenport." He pivoted sharply and bowed in one fluid motion. A stray lock of hair fell dropped in front of his forehead. His navy tailcoat had the effect of making his eyes appear more sapphire than turquoise.

"It is I who must apologize. I'm afraid my call today is more than just a social call." He ran a hand through his hair. "I'm afraid I bring ill tidings, indeed. I was at my club this morning when I overheard several members near me in deep conversation about a scandal in Hyde Park."

Glumly, Aunt Sarah poured herself a cup of tea. Helen's legs grew shaky. She sank into the wingback seat across from her aunt.

"Helen and I were privy to a similar tale during our afternoon shopping sojourn."

"I fear it grows worse." Mr. Marcellus clenched his fists. "I have it on good authority that an enemy of mine has made it his personal mission to ensure that I am identified as the man involved in the incident."

He took several steps to the fireplace and rested his hand upon the mantle. "On the day of the accident, I was seen coming and going from this address. It remains only a matter of time before you will be deduced as the woman in the story. For this, I am deeply sorry."

Helen opened and closed her mouth. Her world was being ripped apart at the seams. She was bitterly angry. Life as a woman was not fair. If she had been granted a supernatural power like the Greek god Zeus, she would have opted to shoot jolts of electricity out of her body.

If she were a man, she'd be able to shrug off the accident. Nobody would think twice about a gentleman assisting a servant. Why was this happening to her?

John's face appeared in her mind's eye. The anger simmered to a low boil. She rubbed the crook of her arm where he had hastily pulled her from harm's way and risked his own life to save hers.

I am thinking only about myself. I have so much to be grateful for, yet here I am wallowing in self-pity.

"This was to be my last chance at making a match. I was foolish to hope that I might finally come away from London a married woman." Helen's lips quivered. "But if this is the price that must be paid for helping John, I'd pay it tenfold."

Trying to put up a strong front was sapping much of her energy reserves. She suddenly grew weary. Her limbs felt heavy, as if she had aged one hundred years. She held her head in her hands and rubbed her temples.

Mr. Marcellus had taken to silently pacing the back of the room, his brow furrowed.

His actions spoke louder than words. She wouldn't be shocked if he sought to leave that very moment.

"Do not give up so easily. Your father and my excellent husband will come up with a plan." Aunt Sarah glanced to the timepiece on the mantle. "They should be arriving home at any moment."

Helen kept her head inclined. "There is no point in risking your own good name. Papa and I will return to Winterbrook. There will always be a hint of scandal associated with me. No intelligent gentleman would consider me worth the risk. The few connections Papa and I might have gained will refuse to receive us. It is useless."

She had her life and her family. For this, she was grateful.

Mr. Marcellus's face had turned a shade of scarlet. His jaw clenched and his shoulders were riddled with tension.

"Helen—" Aunt Sarah began.

She shook her head. "Do not pity me. This is the hand life has dealt me and I shall accept it. The Holbrooks mentioned that I might be taken on as a companion to Miss Holbrooks. Their estate is close enough that I could still visit Papa daily. I'll find happiness watching Lucy and Mary grow into beautiful young ladies in their own right."

A knock sounded at the door. Papa and Uncle William entered, laughing jovially. Their mood, however, abruptly shifted upon their seeing the destitute expressions of the room's occupants.

"Goodness me! What's happened now?" Helen's father exclaimed.

A stray tear escaped down Helen's cheek. No longer able to control her emotions, she jumped out of her seat and rushed over to her father. "Papa. I am as good as ruined. May we return to Winterbrook tonight? I never wish to see London again."

Papa embraced her. She rested her head against the rough cotton of his tailcoat and cried into it.

"Of course, my love. Whatever you wish."

Uncle William cleared his throat. "Mr. Marcellus. Does any of what's happening have to do with why you've standing here as if you wish to break all of the trinkets on my mantelpiece?"

"Yes, sir."

Aunt Sarah clapped her hands together. All of the occupants in the roomed turned their attention to her.

"All of you are overreacting to the situation. Mr. Marcellus, my husband and Mr. Davenport will see you in the study. You will engage in a stiff drink and explain to them the news you have revealed to us."

Aunt Sarah stood and gently placed her hands upon Helen's shoulders and pulled her away from her father.

"Go," she said softly. "Leave her to me. Helen is in shock and has had quite enough excitement for one day. I will see that she calms down and is put to bed. I will join you three in the study shortly to plot our next move."

Knowing better than to try and negotiate with the lady of the house, the men agreed and fled the drawing room.

Mr. Marcellus, however, lingered in the doorway. His voice came out raw. "Miss Davenport, have courage. I will set things right."

He closed the door, and his footsteps echoed against the wooden floors as he walked away.

"Come, Helen. To bed." As if she were a child once

again with her governess, Aunt Sarah held Helen's hand and guided her up to her room.

46

Chapter Six

Helen could not help but appreciate the fine form Mr. Marcellus cut as he alighted from the Greenly carriage at dusk the next evening. His clothing, crafted from the highest quality materials, revealed a physique that might have passed for a Greek statue.

He is Apollo incarnate, indeed.

Papa, Aunt Sarah, and Uncle William exited the carriage. When it was her turn, Helen breathed deeply. Mr. Marcellus extended a gloved hand to hers. Their gazes locked as he assisted her down from the steps, his deep pools of turquoise boring into her.

"Miss Davenport," he acknowledged.

Heat rushed through her body. The pitter-patter of her racing pulse resounded in her ears. How had her body found a way to react to him so quickly?

"Thank you, sir." Her cheeks warmed. She smoothed out her skirt. "It has been quite a long time since either Papa or I have had the honor of attending the opera. I am in your debt for extending an invitation to us this evening."

"Please think nothing of it, Miss Davenport. It is I who should be thanking you and your excellent family for agreeing to attend with me on such short notice. For too long my box has sat empty."

He offered his arm to her and led the party up a set of white marble steps to the entrance to the opera house. Papa, Aunt Sarah, and Uncle William trailed them at a discreet distance, speaking amongst themselves.

"Do you not often attend performances at the theatre?"

Mr. Marcellus shook his head. "Indeed, I do not. I find that I much prefer the quiet of the countryside to Town."

"In this we are alike, sir. For I, too, prefer the natural beauty of the rolling hills, the sounds of the rushing river, and the ability to canter across an open field on my mare. There is no better feeling than that of the cold morning breeze upon one's face."

"From the gleam in your eye, I can see how fond you are of horses and riding." Mr. Marcellus's lips curved up, revealing a set of handsome dimples. "I confess that I find horses to be much more pleasant company than London society."

Helen nodded. "Animals are always preferable to humans."

He chuckled. "Do you keep any animals, Miss Davenport?"

"I do. On my father's estate, I have a feline companion named Mozart."

"Mozart. What a curious name." He raised an eyebrow.

"You would understand if you were to greet him in the flesh. He is a highly vocal fellow. When Mozart is hungry, he ensures that the entirety of the Winterbrook estate is made aware. As if he were a soprano performing an aria, he meows. Loudly."

"My collies, Jupiter and Neptune, will be in good company should they meet your Mozart."

Helen tilted her head to the side. "How so?"

"My dogs are spoiled rotten. Whenever they desire attention, all they need do is bark, and either myself or my staff will shower them with affection. I confess, I have tried my best to ignore them and have attempted to have my gamekeeper train them up, but they are too smart for their own good." Mr. Marcellus shook his head. "I cannot resist a dog who stares at me with sad eyes."

"It is the animals who have trained us," Helen giggled.

"Indeed," he said.

Entering the lobby, Helen noted that it was full of well-dressed ladies and gentlemen clustered in tightly packed circles, entrenched in deep conversation. Similar to navigating a maze of thick yew hedges, Mr. Marcellus guided them through the sea of theatregoers, heading for the quiet of a corner near the rear of the lobby.

"Lord Greenly, Lady Greenly," an acquaintance of Aunt Sarah and Uncle William called out.

Uncle William sighed. "And here I hoped this evening I might be able to avoid speaking business with Lord Montgomery."

"He is a persistent man." Aunt Sarah patted his hand. "Please excuse us."

"If only I had had the foresight to bring a good book with me." Papa's brow furrowed.

"Papa, you are well overdue for a change in scenery." Helen opened her ivory fan and hid a smile. "It is unhealthy for you and Uncle William to shut yourselves in the library night after night and keep such late hours discussing texts from the ancient world."

"You are always welcome to join us, dearest," Papa said.

She was happy to see Papa's long-dormant zest for life return. He and Uncle William were like two schoolboys when they spent time together.

"That invitation is also extended to you, Mr. Marcellus. Your thoughts on what Tacitus wrote in his treatise on—"

"Papa. No more talk of Rome."

He sighed. "Very well."

"We are in luck, Mr. Davenport"—Mr. Marcellus looked to Helen, a trace of amusement in his eyes—"Miss Davenport has not mentioned a ban on any discussion of the Greeks."

Her eyebrow twitched.

In the background a bell sounded, signaling the impending start of the play.

With a look of innocence, Mr. Marcellus suggested, "Shall we go up to the box?"

He offered Helen his arm.

Men.

Inside the theatre, the murmur of human voices was replaced by the cacophony of musical instruments playing notes over one another. A thick set of red velvet curtains, decorated with the crest of the monarch, was drawn closed. Soft golden lights illuminated the interior.

"This is much more agreeable." Papa smiled, seating himself next to Helen. From his pocket, he retrieved a set of silver spectacles and began to review the evening's program. "A comedy in five acts…Shakespeare's *Much Ado About Nothing*. Capital. Capital," he muttered.

How fitting that we are to see a play about the pair of Beatrice and Benedick, tricked into confessing their love for one another, Helen thought.

"I am pleased to see your father approves of the evening's entertainment." Mr. Marcellus relaxed against his seat.

"One can never err when Shakespeare is being performed." She folded her hands atop her lap. "He is, after all, revered as one of the world's foremost English language playwrights."

"I sense you have other feelings, however…"

"I personally would have preferred to see an operetta. I live vicariously through the costumes, the scenery, the music, and the performance. It is the closest I may ever come experiencing what it might be like to travel and see the world."

Helen hoped she hadn't spoken out of turn. Throughout her previous courtship, Mr. Chapman had never wished to hear her thoughts. Instead, he preferred to hear the sound of his own voice.

Mr. Marcellus crossed his legs. "And given the opportunity, where should you like to travel?"

"Everywhere I am allowed." Her eyelids fluttered. "Were I a man, I would have spent at least two years exploring every inch of the continent on my own Grand Tour. I've read Papa's journals countless times."

"The continent is indeed a magnificent place to explore." The corners of his eyes creased. "I can still recall the feeling of joy I had traversing the streets of Herculaneum and Pompeii. Or when my hired guide led me to the ancient Agora of Athens."

Helen's eyelids fluttered. "How dreamy."

He sighed deeply. "I just hope that when the tyrant Napoleon is vanquished, the sights I once enjoyed will remain untouched. War knows no bounds."

Helen shivered. To think that monuments built more than fifteen hundred years ago could be laid to waste by one man and his army both angered and saddened her.

Mr. Marcellus touched her hand. "Come now, Miss Davenport. There should be no long faces tonight. I may yet be proven wrong." He lowered his voice and leaned forward in his seat. "Know this… if we should be inclined to marry, when the war has passed, we will enjoy an extended tour of the continent. Together."

Her pulse raced, and she licked her lips. She could picture herself and Mr. Marcellus cackling wildly as they rode a pair of camels in Egypt with the pyramids of the pharaohs behind them. She could hear the sound of his voice whispering poetry to her as they strolled across one of the many graceful bridges spanning the canals of Venice.

For the first time in her life, Helen saw herself as a married woman. The thought caused her body to tingle with waves of excited energy.

"Truly?" she whispered.

"Yes," he murmured.

Footsteps brought the return of Aunt Sarah and Uncle William to the box. They seated themselves behind her and Mr. Marcellus.

A second bell rang, and the house lights dimmed.

"Excellent, we made it just in time," Uncle William said.

Papa agreed.

Mr. Marcellus removed his hand from Helen's.

The curtain began to rise. The orchestra took up their instruments, but Helen was engaged in studying the profile of Mr. Marcellus.

He has a strong jaw and such defined cheekbones. They would be sharp enough to cut a quill upon.

"Do you find me to be of more interest than the play?" he whispered.

Helen jumped in her seat. Her face burned. "No, Mr. Marcellus, not at all. I… I… I merely was wondering where I might have placed my opera glasses?"

A low rumble came from Mr. Marcellus's throat. "Please. Take mine."

She knew she had no choice but to accept his offer. Even if her own glasses were in fact tucked away in the reticule on her lap.

"Thank you, sir."

She held them up to her eyes and stared straight ahead to the stage, too embarrassed to gauge the reaction of Mr. Marcellus.

And we have only just begun courting. What he must think of me!

~

Throughout the play, as hard as Helen may have tried to focus on the actors on the stage, she found it was much more interesting to watch how Mr. Marcellus reacted to the actors. When he was amused, the corners of his eyes wrinkled ever so slightly, and a pair of dimples appeared. When he was curious, he arched his left eyebrow and scooted forward to the edge of his seat.

Just as she felt she was beginning to be able to read his body language, the play came to an end. Helen snapped her head away from Mr. Marcellus and directed her gaze to the stage.

The audience roared with applause. Like Papa and Uncle William, Mr. Marcellus was quickly on his feet. He gave a blaring whistle and shouted, "Bravo! Bravo!"

Helen and Aunt Sarah gave a more muted, but still appreciative, applause.

"That was excellent. Shakespeare is a comedic genius, indeed," Mr. Marcellus said. He slipped his white gloves onto his hands. "How did you find the play this evening, Miss Davenport? Was it to your liking?"

Helen stood. The muscles in her neck were taut with tension from staring at her suitor. "It was brilliant." She hesitated. "I found the scenery to be lifelike—it successfully transported me to Sicily."

Technically, it is not a fib. Except that I was engaged in watching Mr. Marcellus instead of the play. Thinking about a Grand Tour did transport me to Italy, just not Sicily, where the play is set.

"And Mr. Christensen, the actor playing Benedict? Was his delivery not perfectly sharp and dripping with sarcasm?"

Their party left Mr. Marcellus's box and slowly descended the grand steps to the lobby of the theatre as he launched into an enthusiastic recount of the evening. Helen listened intently, nodding every few minutes. This was the most animated she had seen the man.

When he is relaxed, he is even more handsome. He appears so much younger and more carefree.

As they joined the crush waiting for the carriages to arrive, Papa draped Helen's cape around her shoulders. "My dear, you're rather mute."

Helen blinked twice. "I'm sorry, Papa, I suppose I'm just a bit fatigued after the excitement of *Much Ado About Nothing.*"

Uncle William patted her hand. "Not to worry, Helen. Our carriage should be arriving momentarily."

Butterflies fluttered in her stomach. Was the night to end so soon? She wanted to spend more time in the company of Mr. Marcellus.

As if reading her mind, Mr. Marcellus sighed. "Just as well. All good things must come to an end." From his pocket, he removed a watch fob and reviewed the time. "It's later than I thought. Unfortunately, I have two appointments rather early in the morning that cannot be put off."

Uncle William also checked the time. "What a shame, Mr. Marcellus, we would have loved to invite you over for a night cap. You are always welcome at number twelve Curzon Street. If you are not so inclined to call upon Helen, Hugh and I would welcome your company."

"William," Aunt Sarah admonished.

Papa chuckled.

"Will you at the very least let our carriage convey you home?" Uncle William asked.

Mr. Marcellus shook his head. "There is no need. I reside close and will return by foot.

I will say my farewells to you here."

"Very well, sir," Uncle William nodded.

The Greenly carriage slowed as it pulled to the head of the parade. Helen rubbed the palms of her hands against the skirt of her dress.

"Here we are." Uncle William extended his arm to Aunt Sarah.

"Miss Davenport, if I might escort you to the carriage," Mr. Marcellus said.

Papa winked and trailed behind them.

Taking hold of Mr. Marcellus's arm, Helen moved in closer to his body. It radiated with heat. "The next time we attend a performance together, I will endeavor to ensure that it is an operetta," he said.

Helen's cheeks warmed. "Oh, Mr. Marcellus, I would be more than happy to see any performance. It does not have to be limited to an opera."

His eyes danced under the light of the torches. "I will keep that in mind."

"Will you call upon me on the morrow?"

"Alas, as much I would rather spend time in your company, I fear that I will be passing the entirety of the day in the office of my solicitor. However, if I finish early, I will make every effort to call upon you."

Helen nodded. "Then the next time we shall meet will be at the Woodrow ball."

He grinned. "Indeed. I am looking forward to dancing two sets with you."

They reached the carriage. Bringing her gloved hand to his lips, he placed a gentle, chaste kiss upon it. His eyes locked on to hers. Internally, she shivered in delight.

"Good night, Miss Davenport."

He handed her up to the carriage.

"Good night, Mr. Marcellus."

Her hand remained in his a moment longer than necessary as she slid into position. The door slammed shut.

Uncle William tapped on the top of the carriage. "Walk on."

Mr. Marcellus backed away and stood with his hands behind his back as she watched his form disappear from sight, counting down the moments until they could be together again.

Chapter Seven

Helen stood with her family just outside the entry door to Woodrow Manor's ballroom, site of the evening's festivities. Wax poured down the flickering candles illuminating the path. Helen adjusted her elbow-length gloves, wishing dearly she could remove them. The fabric was itchy against her skin and the fit was too confining.

"Aunt, are you certain attending the ball tonight is a good idea?" she murmured.

"I am positive. We mustn't act as if we are aware that the status quo has changed. William and Mr. Marcellus have carefully sent out discrete inquiries about town. There is not a single whisper of your name being mentioned in connection to you-know-what."

Yet. I hope this plan goes out without a hitch. It seems like a stretch to make it appear as if Mr. Marcellus has been courting me since I arrived to town.

Aunt Sarah whispered into Helen's ear, "Stand tall, shoulders square, and do not let your guard down. The matchmaking mamas of the Ton are like sharks circling their prey. At the first sign of weakness, they will make their move."

She reviewed Helen's appearance one final time. "As far as they are concerned, until there is a proposal formally made to you by Mr. Marcellus, they will try to turn his eyes towards their daughters." Her aunt smiled. "Now, try to enjoy the evening. There is no need to stress. No matter what, Mr. Marcellus has promised Hugh and William he would do the honorable thing and marry you."

The palms of Helen's hands grew clammy.

They had spent the better part of three visits together and she still knew practically nothing about the man. What was his given name? Where was his estate? Did he have any family? The questions swirled through her brain.

All that I have to go on is that he is well read and able to engage Papa and Uncle William in debates.

Her heart began to beat at a quicker pace. When Mr. Marcellus was around, Helen found herself unable to think clearly. She felt safe, warm, and protected. She couldn't put her finger on it, but there was something about the man that evoked an entire new set of sensations within her. She'd always been proud of her ability to be sensible when it came to men, but with Mr. Marcellus, it was not her head that did the speaking, but her heart.

Aunt Sarah cleared her throat. "William, Hugh, we are ready."

Helen's father, dressed in a coat of emerald green,

extended his arm to her. "Miss Davenport, you are a vision."

She squeezed her father's hand. "Thank you, Papa."

Her aunt and uncle slowly descended the stairs ahead of them. Entering the ballroom, she had never felt more beautiful, in a light green gown complete with an embroidered gold sash.

Musicians played upon their instruments. Four and twenty couples formed two lines and danced in formation, jumping lightly on the balls of their feet. Hushed conversations took place in small groups of four and five.

There were officers in crisp red coats with gold braiding, gentlemen in dark-colored tailcoats, and women in light-colored gowns. Atop many of the women's heads, fashionable feathers represented every shade imaginable.

Helen was especially grateful Aunt Sarah abhorred that particular trend. Instead, two sets of ringlets framed her heart-shaped face, with the remainder of her hair wound in a stylish braided hairstyle.

Their party of four settled in the corner of the room. Aunt Sarah removed a white feathered fan from her reticule. "It is always so stuffy when there are so many people in a room."

"This is the grandest ball I have ever attended." Helen's eyes searched the room, which was not yet full. "I thought the Woodrow family invited several hundred guests."

"We are unfashionably early, my dear. Mr. Marcellus will find you when he arrives. Of that, I have no doubt." Her father chuckled. "Until then, best you enjoy the ball."

Aunt Sarah huddled closer to her. In a hushed tone, she said, "I wanted us here early so you would know friend versus foe. Over there with the blue peon feather is Lady Ringwald. She is like Lady Woodrow in that she has a knack for fishing for information from a person. Be mindful of how you answer her questions. To her left in the orange is Lady Johnson. Her husband is a member of the House of Lords with William."

Helen's mind attempted to keep up with the steady stream of names and faces that Aunt Sarah mentioned to her. She must have been made aware of at least fifty at last count.

"Are there any other ladies we may consider as friendly?" Helen removed her own fan and covered her mouth.

"Mrs. Smyth in the muted yellow gown, to the left of the orchestra, will ensure you make the acquaintances of all the right people. A few select introductions shall carry you far. My Thomas is married to Mrs. Smyth's second-eldest daughter."

A gentleman with bright red hair and a royal-blue tailcoat approached. He bowed. "Lord Greenly, I do not believe I've made the acquaintance of this remarkable creature you've brought with you this evening. Will you be so kind as to introduce us?"

Is he speaking of me?

Helen sucked in air.

She was never one of the chosen few who received a gentleman's attention. The gentlemen always sought out those who were making their entry into society. Not those sitting on the shelf, like her.

"Mr. Palmer, I trust your father is well. This is my

niece, Miss Davenport, and her excellent father, Mr. Davenport," Uncle William said.

"Mr. Davenport. Miss Davenport," Mr. Palmer greeted them both. "If your dance card is not yet full, may I reserve two sets with you this evening?"

Helen fanned herself. Her body grew heated. "You may."

"May I be bold enough to ask if you have already been claimed for the opening set?"

"I have not."

Mr. Palmer clapped his hands together. "Capital. I'll come and collect you when it is

our time. If you would please excuse me.

Helen watched Mr. Palmer's retreating form. "And here I thought I'd only be dancing two sets this evening." She shook her head in disbelief.

"Helen, you are the guest of an earl." Aunt Sarah returned the fan to her reticule. "By the evening's end, your poor feet shall be unable to fit in your shoes due to all the dancing. We might even require a strong footman to carry you to the carriage."

Helen tilted her head to the side. "Do you really think that's possible?"

Uncle William chuckled. "My wife is never wrong."

Society was so strange. Having just one connection to signal to others she was worthy of their acquaintance had changed her fortunes.

In the span of a week in London, she had gone from hopeless to being courted by Mr. Marcellus. In her combined previous seasons, she'd relegated herself to watching the jovial dancing from afar. Few suitors had interest in a woman with a dowry of only five thousand pounds when there were heiresses with ten, fifteen, and even twenty thousand available.

By the time the gentlemen seeking a wife turned their heads towards whomever was still "on the market," Papa would usually be low on funds. They would have to close up their rented accommodations early and return to Winterbrook. The sad truth was that the older she grew, the less inclined a gentleman was to make an offer to her. They never want the "leftovers."

As Lady Woodrow signaled to the orchestra for the dancing to begin, Mr. Palmer returned from the far side of the room and claimed Helen's hand. "Miss Davenport, I believe this set is mine."

With a light touch, he escorted her to their places. They stood across from one another as the musicians struck up a tune. The partners bowed to one another, and in groups of four, walked in a circle clockwise. Helen giggled. She felt like a young maid of sixteen once again, wracking her memory for the dance's pattern.

Does Mr. Marcellus care for dancing? What type of partner would he be?

Helen's stomach clenched. There were only three sets remaining and Mr. Marcellus still had yet to make his entrance. She recognized the closing notes of the quadrille.

Her chest grew uncomfortably tight. Had Mr. Marcellus changed his mind? Maybe she wasn't the sort of woman he envisioned as a proper wife after all. She forced the ends of her lips to remain upright.

At least I haven't wasted too much time pining for him. I should never have set my hopes so high.

Her father's worried eyes appraised her. Helen hurriedly swept her feathered fan in front of her face, not letting him see her distress. Aunt Sarah pursed her lips. Uncle William checked the time on his watch fob. They continued to speak of books and neutral topics.

Why are they so nervous? Or is there something that they are keeping from me?

Her mind began to envision one unfortunate scenario after another. She needed air.

"Papa, my throat's become parched. I shall return shortly." She slipped away before he could reply.

Weaving her way around the parties of chatting guests, she maintained a close distance to the wall.

Keeping her ears sharp, she listened to snippets of their conversations.

"The Cliff Household can certainly expect a plethora of callers over the coming days."

"Miss Lyons has her cap set on Lord Burley, the Earl of Ashwood. She'll have a nasty surprise waiting when she finds out the sorry state of his finances."

"Shall we make a wager? Which household will announce an engagement first, the Cliffs or Hunters?"

Her eyes traveled to the ballroom's door one last time. She breathed deeply.

Why am I so bothered by Mr. Marcellus's lack of appearance? It is not as if I hold a tendre for him or anyone else.

She reached the refreshment table, and just as she was about to help herself to a glass of lemonade, she froze. The temperature of the room dropped ten degrees, and her stays became uncomfortably tight. Standing a mere few feet from her was Mr. Chapman.

Had he seen her? Could she still avoid him? Quickly backing away, Helen kept her chin lowered and snapped her fan open.

The sound of the crack caught the attention of her former suitor.

"Miss Davenport. I'm shocked to see you here," Mr. Chapman said, his voice sardonic.

Chapter Eight

Helen turned and curtsied, burying her discountenance beneath a forced smile. "Mr. Chapman."

Behind him stood a gaggle of three other gentlemen. Helen, however, kept refusing to meet their gazes.

Mr. Chapman scoffed lightly. "Men, you would do well to steer clear of this chit. She lacks any breeding or connections to speak of and is doomed to the future of—"

She clenched the base of her fan tighter. Her body warmed.

"—a penniless spinster," he sputtered derisively.

She took three steps backward and brushed the edge of the table. Mr. Chapman inched closer to her, his breath reeking of strong spirits. "Why, I even heard from the Davenports' neighbors that the chit has made inquiries to them about her entering service as their gov—"

"Chapman, that is quite enough. Your vile tongue

has been loosened by strong spirits. You are clearly not in a fit state to be among gentile company. Apologize and move away from the lady."

That voice! The rich blend of baritone, clout, and dominance could only belong to one person.

Mr. Marcellus! He's arrived!

Helen lifted her chin to watch Mr. Marcellus, dressed in a navy-colored coat, cream-striped waistcoat, and black breeches, close the space between them in three powerful strides. Like a tempest storm, she could feel the waves of anger rolling off his person.

"What is she to you?" The sneer in Mr. Chapman's voice was palpable. He looked over his shoulder.

Mr. Marcellus kept his frosty gaze on Mr. Chapman's face, his jaw muscles clenched. "Miss Davenport is among the most handsome, accomplished women of my acquaintance and the woman I am courting."

Yes, Mr. Chapman, you heard correctly!

Helen trembled, knowing that she would quickly become a target and enemy number one for the matchmaking mamas of the Ton.

"You want the worthless woman?" Mr. Chapman's face contorted in a grimace. "Take her. Please."

He pushed her towards Mr. Marcellus, whose strong arms caught and steadied her. The rich scent of sandalwood and cinnamon tickled her nose.

With a rush of adrenaline, she uttered, "Ego sim nequam."

I am not worthless. Doubtless the blockhead won't understand Latin.

One of Mr. Chapman's friends inclined his head to

Mr. Marcellus. "Apologies, sir. We weren't aware of your connection to the lady. I'll ensure that Chapman won't be bothering either of you again tonight."

"You have my thanks," he said.

They pulled Mr. Chapman out of the room.

Mr. Marcellus offered Helen his arm, clearing his throat. "Miss Davenport, I've come to claim you for our set."

She accepted his arm, itching to be as far away from the scene of the incident as possible.

"Are you well, Miss Davenport?" he asked in a low tone.

"I am fine. You have my thanks for defending me, sir." Her tone came out clipped.

"You are angry with me," he said, his turquoise eyes gleaming with regret. "I'm sorry I have arrived so late. My horse threw a shoe on the way to the ball. I misjudged how long it would take to find another mount."

"I'm cross, but I am angrier still with myself for lacking the courage to speak up against my former suitor." She kept her voice tight, willing herself to breathe and not let her emotions overcome her.

She closed her eyes, counted to five, and breathed deeply. When she opened them, she upturned the corners of her lips. "I will not let the encounter with Mr. Chapman spoil my evening. I am here for the explicit purpose of learning if we might suit as a couple."

Mr. Marcellus's face brightened. Helen soaked in the dimples that appeared on his face as he smiled. Was it healthy for her to already be developing affection for how his eyes twinkled?

"Let us dance," he said.

They took up positions across from one another, their bodies wrapped in a gentle embrace as the musicians took up their instruments. They bowed to one another, and he took her hand. Through the thin fabric of her gloves, she could feel the heat from his hand. It was so much larger than her own. He moved lightly on his feet, cutting an excellent figure.

Whispers sprung from different areas of the room. Women shot Helen curious glances as she and Mr. Marcellus finished their second set. The cloak of confidence she'd donned earlier was rapidly fraying at the seams.

"For the last four Seasons, I've been able to hide in plain sight. I was well practiced in the art of being a wallflower. And now…" She shivered.

Mr. Marcellus squeezed her hand in support. "And now you shall be given the attention you rightly deserve. There will be no more hiding, Miss Davenport. You were not born to fit in. You were born to stand out."

Heat seared her cheeks. "Begging your pardon, sir. I may be a gentlewoman, but I have little to offer by way of beauty. I am as plain as the nose on my face. You must be speaking about one of the other lovely women in the room."

"I disagree." Mr. Marcellus frowned. "You have a natural beauty that radiates from the inside out. It's a beauty that lights up the darkest of nights. Appearances will fade with the passage of time, but kindness, compassion, and a wit as sharp as yours will long remain."

Her heart made a few happy roars, but she quickly cautioned herself. Mr. Chapman had also offered her similar compliments.

"I've had my fill of dancing for the evening. What do you say to a stroll in the garden?" Mr. Marcellus glanced around before meeting her gaze again. "The hall is filled with too many prying eyes and ears."

"I would like nothing better." The calmness that poured out with her voice surprised her.

He extended his hand to her, his eyes never leaving hers. Her pulse began to race. They walked in silence as he led her out of the hall and down the staircase. Helen marveled at how Mr. Marcellus retained his manners and took care to acknowledge each person they passed.

I am a bundle of nerves, but Mr. Marcellus acts as if he is immune to the whisperings. How does one ever grow used to such a thing?

Arriving at the garden, a cold breeze cooled her overly warm body. Helen smiled as she breathed in the sweet smell of the white roses. Overhead, the moon appeared from behind a curtain of dark clouds, its silver rays filtering through the tree branches. Water trickled from a small fountain.

"Gardens are quiet, and one of the few places that I find I can hear myself think," Mr. Marcellus said.

"I agree. There are many times at Winterbrook that I've sought the solace of the gardens." She breathed in the scent of the nearby roses. "Tell me, does your home have a garden?"

They sat on a bench beneath an arbor coated in red, pink, and white flowers.

"The formal gardens at my country estate, Springwood Hall, are tended by my large staff of gardeners. My grandfather was an avid horticulturalist and devoted much of his later life to creating hybrid breeds of flowers. Roses were his specialty. While other gardens grow and die with the seasons, Springwood is blessed with blooming plants year-round."

Mr. Marcellus seemed to be lost in his thoughts. His eyes glazed over. "My true love, however, is Springwood's wildflower gardens. I've always thought nature is at its best when it's left untouched and untamed. I enjoy the mystery of seeing what and where plants will bloom."

Helen pictured an open field with thousands of orange, pink, blue, and yellow flowers opening their petals to the first rays of morning light. With a thin layer of fog wafting over the plants, she and Mr. Marcellus would ride their horses through the brush, releasing thousands of butterflies into the air.

"Where exactly is Springwood Hall? You mentioned in our first meeting you were from the north."

"Yorkshire, not far from the Dales. On a clear day, the view of the rolling hills and mighty rivers is endless."

Mr. Marcellus recounted his experiences exploring the region and why he thought the Dales of Yorkshire were much more enjoyable than the Peak District of Derbyshire. Helen felt as if she'd been transported to Yorkshire from the way he vividly described the landscape to her.

"And what of your library, sir?"

"As I recounted to your father a few days ago, it is still very much a work in progress. My late father had grand ambitions for the estate and the library, but unfortunately, with his untimely demise, his vision never materialized." His voice grew quiet.

Helen inclined her gaze to his, waiting to see a flash of pain, or some other sign of anguish. However, Mr. Marcellus remained unreadable, his emotions tucked neatly away.

"It is never easy to lose a parent. My own excellent mother passed from this world when I was but a child. I have few memories of her, but those that I do have, I cherish."

"I am sorry." Mr. Marcellus's eyes flickered with remorse. "I lost both of my parents and my sister in a terrible carriage accident when I was two and twenty."

Helen's heart broke.

To lose all whom he loved at once. She don't know how he was able to go on. Papa was her world. She couldn't imagine him being there one minute, and the next gone.

They sat in silence for several moments.

Staring into the flicker of the flames dancing through the window, Mr. Marcellus ever so slightly nodded his head.

"I have not spoken of them in more than six years." He stood and paced. "In many ways, it is as if they are still here with us. Our London townhouse remains as it was the night of the accident. I could never muster the courage to pack it up. My sister's ballgown still rests upon her bed, waiting for her to dress. My mother's earrings are atop the jewel case on her dressing table."

His breath hitched. "They were returning from a day out, shopping on Bond Street when it happened…" His body shuddered.

That made Mr. Marcellus eight and twenty. How old was his sister? Was she of a similar age to Helen? Papa urged her to wait until she was eight and ten to make her debut. Six years. It was not so very long ago. London must hold many painful reminders for Mr. Marcellus.

A sudden, horrible thought struck her. Helen laced her fingers through his. "Have you been alone this entire time?"

"Yes. I have no other family."

Slowly, she rose to her feet. Aware that she was breaking every single rule of propriety, she slowly wrapped her arms around him and hugged him tightly. He melted into her warm embrace. She felt the heat of his body.

Slowly, his hands trailed up her body, from the small of her back and up to her face. He gently moved a stray lock of hair behind her ear, licking his lips.

"You are so beautiful, Miss Davenport. How is it that a chap like me was lucky enough to encounter such an ethereal vision?"

Her eyes closed. The air smelled of florals, wax from the candles, and sandalwood. They moved into one another. Her lips parted.

Suddenly, a shrill voice screeched, "Mama, we must be the first ones to find him!" Labored breathing and heavy footsteps brought a woman in an ivory white gown out to the garden.

Helen and Mr. Marcellus hastily jumped back from one another. He put a finger to his lips and signaled for her to crouch down in the shadows behind the potted rosebush. She splayed a hand on her chest, her heart beating a mile a minute.

The lady stomped her feet. "Where is he? We've looked everywhere!"

Helen made out the curvy silhouette of a shorter woman wearing a red feather. "Sweetling, come inside before you catch a chill. The man will not be out of doors, where he could be easily compromised. He's been smart enough to stay away from society until now."

"You're right, Mama." The woman in the ivory gown crossed her arms, but lingered in the doorway. "I just can't comprehend why it has only just become common knowledge that the man parading around as Mr. Marcellus is in fact the Duke of Willowbard!"

A gloved hand covered Helen's mouth as she gasped.

Mr. Marcellus was a duke—one of the most richest and most powerful men in the country. He had been lying to her the entire time. She could not trust him.

Her body stiffened, and she clenched her fists.

The eyes of the lady in the ivory dress swept the garden one last time. "Mark my words, I will be a duchess if it's the last thing I do! Nobody is going to stand in my way."

The mother and daughter headed back towards the ballroom, their voices becoming quieter until Helen could only hear the sound of running water and heavy breathing. She was once again alone with Mr. Marcellus.

As he removed his hand from her mouth and slowly came to a standing position, he sputtered, "Miss Davenport. I can explain—"

"No. You've done quite enough for the evening, sir!" Helen backed away. "Mr. Marcellus, or whatever your real name is, consider our courting at an end. I will not consent to marry a man who seeks to lie to me."

"Miss Davenport, I have *never* lied to you."

Helen turned her back to him. "I ask you, then, good sir, what is your *real* name?"

He winced. "I am Robert Anthony Lily, the sixth Duke of Willowbard."

"How could I have been so blind?" She shook her head. "Just as I allowed myself to begin to develop some type of feelings for you."

"Miss Davenport. Helen…"

Salty tears began to roll down her cheeks and into her mouth.

A second chorus of female voices approached the garden doorway.

They both froze.

"Have you heard about that country upstart Miss Davenport? The room cannot stop speaking about it! She's penniless. Mr. Chapman confirmed she has a dowry of only one thousand pounds."

"And she fancies herself able to catch a duke!" The women cackled.

"I heard that she is not even gently bred. Her mother was a lowly maid whom her father took a fancy to."

"It's no wonder she's been on the shelf for four Seasons!"

Helen could not stand to listen to them any longer. She wanted to yell and scream, but knew little good would come of it. Leaving the stunned duke and vile gossip behind, she fled the garden.

"Was that Miss Davenport? I think she heard you!"

"Who cares, look! It is the duke!"

Chapter Nine

The ball was ending. Guests slowly moved from the ballroom towards the entry hall to the long line of waiting carriages. Sticking to the shadows, Helen took care to avoid being seen and sought refuge inside one of one of the ladies' retiring rooms. Plush red couches were strategically placed along the walls. A roaring fire crackled. The candles lighting the room had burned low.

Helen breathed hard and rested her gloved palms against the marble countertop of a side table.

So far, she had been spared being identified as the woman from Hyde Park, but after tonight, it wouldn't be long until that changed, especially if Mr. Chapman sought to enact revenge against Helen and her father. Her reputation was all that she had.

Her lips quivered.

I was reckless in the garden with Mr. Marcellus. What if we were seen?

A pair of footsteps resounded against the wooden

floor. "Helen," Aunt Sarah called out. She glanced up to see her aunt's eyes dark with worry. Aunt Sarah quickly closed the distance between them. "Mr. Marcellus was concerned and asked your father, Uncle William, and I to find you. He said you had run away. What's happened?"

Her body shook. "Oh, Aunt, everything is wrong." She sobbed into Aunt Sarah's shoulder.

Aunt Sarah's arms wrapped around her. "Shh… cry. Cry as hard and long as you need to, my dear. Then, when there are no more tears left to let out, we will chat." She rubbed circles soothingly on Helen's upper back, and as if she were a child, tenderly rocked her back and forth.

All of the pent-up anger, fear, sorrow, and hurt erupted from her body just as the River Lea had breached the banks and flooded Winterbrook's fields the year before, consuming everything in its path.

She cried until the skin around her eyes was so dry and raw, it felt as though it might crack. The fire burned low. Few candles in the room remained lit. Neither woman was aware of how much time had passed.

It was Aunt Sarah who finally breached the silence. "Helen, I was never blessed with a daughter of my own, but if I had been, I imagine that she might be like you. I want you to know that I love you so much and that you can always tell me anything."

Aunt Sarah was the only mother she had ever truly known. She had taken Helen under her wing and guided her above and beyond the role of a godmother.

Helen blinked. "I love you too, Aunt." Feeling more in control of herself, she breathed deeply. "I've made a blunder of everything that you, Papa, and Uncle William had hoped for me."

Helen recounted what had taken place in garden—her row with Mr. Marcellus and overhearing the vile gossip of the gaggle of women.

"You must not give any credit to a single word uttered by those ladies. It is their jealousy speaking."

"I know that now, Aunt." She spoke in an even tone. "And I promise, I won't."

"And your gentleman suitor?"

Helen sighed. "I was so angry with the man for withholding information from me, for being late, and for making me feel as if he was using me." She blew out a long breath "But the truth of the matter is that even after all that, I still find myself caring for him. He brings a smile to my face when he walks into the room." Her cheeks burned. "I have these strange sensations running through my body when he's close to me. I've never felt that way about another person before."

Aunt Sarah covered her mouth with her hand and smiled at her encouragingly. "Those strange sensations that you are describing to me… Helen, that's the beginning of what it feels like to be in love." Aunt Sarah's eyes danced. "It was the same when I first met your uncle. Right here"—she touched her heart—"there was a lightness and a strong sense of joy that filled my body. With time, our bond has only continued to grow deeper and stronger. I sense the same will be true of you and your young man."

"I wish it were so." Helen lowered her head. "But in

the heat of the moment, I told Mr. Marcellus that our courtship was at an end."

"The situation is not nearly as dire as you have presented it."

"You believe so?" Helen's gaze met her aunt's.

"I don't believe Mr. Marcellus will be willing to let you go so easily. When he materialized in the ballroom, he was a man who was in anguish and clearly concerned for your well-being. He even offered to lead the search himself and would have had your papa not explained that you have always preferred to have time and space to calm yourself."

Her aunt's words gave her a spark of hope.

"I hope he will call on us soon."

"I would be shocked if he did not." Aunt Sarah smiled at her encouragingly. "Open your heart. Let it guide you. There are so many things about the world you are just on the verge of discovering. What do the writings of Homer teach you?"

Her aunt was beginning to sound like Papa. A ghost of a smile appeared on Helen's lips. "Life is about the delight of the battle, the adventures one has en route to the final destination."

"Yes," Aunt Sarah said, nodding. Straightening their skirts, she ensured Helen was presentable before they returned to the men.

Although she had not arrived home until three in the morning, sleep evaded Helen. She tossed and turned, and finally, shortly after dawn, gave up the premise completely. Wrapping herself in a silk robe, she perched herself atop the window seat.

Any woman in her position would be celebrating their ability to climb and establish themselves at the top of the social ladder, but that was one of the last things she'd ever consider. What women wanted to have all the freedoms they held dear taken away from them?

As a duchess, every word she spoke would be scrutinized. The small family of servants she'd known her entire life would be replaced by those who treated her in a manner befitting a duchess rather than as a friend.

She pulled her knees to her chest and rested her forehead upon them. She pictured Mr. Marcellus and his glowing smile. His thoughtfulness in gifting her a rare book. She could see his full lips and almost smell the roses from the garden where they had very nearly kissed.

I suppose the trouble would be worth it IF I were to have a man who loved and cherished me.

Steadily, the sun's morning rays emerged from the horizon. Higher and higher it rose, until all traces of the night had disappeared. Aware that her maid Patsy had waited late for her mistress to return the night prior, Helen opted to dress herself. When the task was complete, she tiptoed out her bedroom door.

"Miss Davenport, you are up early this morning." She jumped. Watson stood erect, with his hands behind his back.

She splayed a hand on her chest. "Good morning, Watson. You've given me a fright."

"My sincerest apologies, miss." He inclined his head.

"Mr. Davenport and Lord and Lady Greenly are not expected to be up for several hours yet. Shall I have a tray sent to your room?"

Helen glanced to the staircase. "Actually, I had wondered if you might be privy to whether John is awake or not."

"Indeed, he is, Miss Davenport."

"I shall like to visit with him. Can you have a tray prepared for the two of us?"

The base of Watson's neck colored the lightest shade of pale pink. Helen blinked twice.

Do my eyes deceive me, or is Watson embarrassed?

"Master John has already broken his fast. However, I shall personally see that a tray is prepared and sent up for you." From behind his back, Watson revealed a small book. "If you would be so inclined to read to him, Master John would welcome hearing selections from this."

Helen accepted the book from his hands. Her fingers brushed over the worn cover of a 1760 copy of *A Description of Three Hundred Beasts.*

Watson, you old softy. Your secret is safe with me.

"Certainly." She tucked the book under her arm. "I shall leave it with John for you to collect when I finish the visit."

"Very good, Miss Davenport." Watson disappeared from Helen's sight through a side door, down the servant's staircase.

Turning tail, she picked up the hem of her skirt and ascended the stairs to the first bedroom on the right. She rapped softly on the door, and John's voice called for her to enter. She pushed the door fully open and entered the room.

"Miss Davenport! I've been hoping that you might stop by. Watson mentioned that you attended a ball last evening and that I should expect Lord Greenly and Mr. Davenport to sit with me much later than normal." John wiggled his way up out from the cocoon of blankets. "Which book do you have with you?"

Helen was thrilled to see John looking almost normal. His hair was disheveled and his face coated in a thin, uneven layer of facial hair. His eyes shone bright and clear, full of curiosity.

Helen's lips turned up. "Watson recommended this." She held up the book.

John's face lit up at seeing the scarlet cover. "Brilliant. We were just reading about the panthers and lions. Watson makes the best animal sounds."

She filed the information away and lowered herself into the chair next to his bedside. A vase of yellow lilies brightened the room, matching the color of her day dress.

The spine of the book cracked as she opened it. Propping the book against the side of the bed, she began to read. "Of all the beasts of Africa, the giraffe boasts a neck that extends to the tips of the tallest trees…"

Helen slammed her book shut.

The newspaper in Papa's hands rustled. He lowered it and appraised his daughter. "Helen, you are beginning to resemble one of the beasts from John's book. What has you so agitated?"

"Papa, the more my mind wanders, the more I am left to wonder if the rumors spreading about myself and Mr. Marcellus were spread on purpose rather than by coincidence."

Methodically, Papa folded the newspaper and placed it on the table. He folded his hands.

"Last evening, I overheard a group of women speaking about how Mr. Chapman had let it slip about my small dowry." Helen rubbed her temples. "I cannot help but wonder if it was he who—"

A knock interrupted their exchange. Watson opened it to announce the arrival of His Grace, the Duke of Willowbard.

Chapter Ten

Helen's head rose to the sight of Mr. Marcellus. He paused in the doorway to remove his hat, gloves, and walking stick and passed them to Watson. Dark shadows appeared under his eyes. Though he was impeccably groomed, she could sense his exhaustion.

Helen and her father stood and greeted him.

"Mr. Davenport, Miss Davenport." He bowed.

"Mr. Marcellus, lad, please join us. The tea is still warm." Papa gestured to the extra place setting.

Strange that she and Papa were both aware they should refer to him as Your Grace, but neither of them seemed able to break the habit of calling him any name but Mr. Marcellus.

"Thank you for receiving me straightaway. Regrettably, I'm unable to stay long. There is still much to be done. The whisperings of our entanglement in Hyde Park *have* indeed come to light."

Her gaze met the duke's. The intense swirling turquoise reminded her of the wild, stormy sea. "When?" she asked.

He shifted his weight from foot to foot. "I heard it departing the ball last evening and once more en route to my solicitor's office this afternoon."

Papa removed his glasses and rubbed his eyes. "It appears we have run out of time, Helen. You must marry."

From his pocket, Mr. Marcellus removed a set of rolled documents. "As we discussed a few days ago, sir, I've had a marriage settlement drawn up. Here is what I am prepared to settle upon for Miss Davenport."

He slid the documents across the table to Papa.

Helen's throat grew dry. "You still wish to offer for me? Even after last evening?"

"I stand by what I said the day we met. I am a gentleman. I will do whatever is in my power to do right by you. Regardless of how you perceived our discussion last evening"—He glanced to the side at Papa.—"I've come to care for you a great deal, Miss Davenport. I believe we would suit one another very well indeed."

Papa let out a low whistle. "You are too generous."

"May I?" she asked quizzically.

Mr. Marcellus nodded.

Papa offered the papers to Helen. "This sum is too much." Her mouth formed the shape of an O. "Thirty thousand pounds for me and ten thousand for each future child?"

Mr. Marcellus rubbed the nape of his neck. "I

wanted to ensure that my future family is well provided for. Should we welcome any daughters into our midst, they will each receive additional sums for their dowries. I am a very wealthy man, and I want my funds to go towards my most valuable asset—my family."

Helen glanced to her father. "Papa, might I have a few words with Mr. Marcellus? Alone?"

Mr. Davenport pushed his chair back, stood, and tucked the newspaper under his arm. "I shall be in the hall if you require me."

Helen stood, her body quivering. "Mr. Marcellus, I have wanted to offer you my sincerest apologies for my behavior last night. It was unsightly of me to—"

"Miss Davenport." He claimed her hand. "Do. Not. Apologize."

Her mouth opened and closed.

"For so long, I have wanted… I had hoped to find a woman who would want me as a husband in every sense of the word. A woman who would be able to see beyond the titles I inherited at birth."

He brought a hand up to her face and brushed a stray lock of hair away from her eyes.

"I was endeared with you from the moment I watched you take command of caring for Master John when any other woman may have fainted away. I see you as a woman who will challenge me intellectually, a woman who will be my partner in life, and a woman who may even grow to love me."

He placed her hand on his over his firm, broad chest. The wool of his tailcoat was rough against her fingers, the rhythmic drumming of his heart powerful. "My heart beats for you."

They moved in close to one another. Interlacing her fingers with his, she methodically brought his other hand up to her own heart. It dwarfed her own. "I think you have already captured my heart." Her body grew warm.

"Last night, I was terrified of all of the unknowns…" she said. "Of all that I might have to give up, and by the possibility of what the future might bring. But I see now that I have been blinded. I should have looked to what I was gaining…"

They were now only millimeters apart. Helen smelled the scent of his lavender shaving soap. "A friend and a husband who will walk through life with me every step of the way. I will never be alone. And once more… I will be loved."

Mr. Marcellus brought her hand to his lips and gazed longingly into her eyes. Getting down onto one knee, he asked, "Miss Davenport. Will you do me the great honor of consenting to become my wife?"

"Yes, I will."

He leapt up and wrapped his own arms around her, spinning her in a joyful circle. Her heart skipped a beat. In that moment, Helen knew that their marriage would be one full of laughter, love, children, and many happy years together.

He cupped her cheeks. "Now that we are an engaged couple, in private, may I call you by your given name?"

"I would expect nothing less from you." Helen eagerly nodded. "And you, sir? How shall I address you?

Robert? Your Grace? Willowbard? Marcellus? There are quite a few names you carry."

His lips twisted. "For most of my life, Marcellus has been my nickname. I have always been drawn to Roman history. My schoolmates thought it fitting I be given a Roman name. Among close friends, it's become the name I prefer to keep. But if you would be so inclined, when it is just us, I should like to be Robert to you."

In a hushed tone, she tested his preferred name. "Robert. How well that sounds."

"My mother was the last person to ever call me that."

She inclined her head. "Do you think she would approve of me? I am a woman with a man's education. I am not the type of woman whom a duke might traditionally seek out."

"To Hades with society." He rolled his eyes. "I would like to think my mama would be proud I have chosen a bride who fulfills me and goes against the status quo. There is a reason I prefer the country to Town."

He was only making Helen fall for him more, as a country girl born and bred.

"May we have Papa come and stay at Springwood Hall with us for long lengths of time?" She walked her fingers up his arm. "I cannot bear to be parted from him."

"I certainly hope so. I'm an Oxford man. He's a Cambridge man. I require constant debates from the Cambridge riffraff to keep me in check and my mind sharp." Helen rested her head on his shoulder. "You may also plan for us to spend much time at Winterbrook."

She let out a large squeal and hugged him tightly again. "Thank you. Thank you. Thank you a thousand times, Robert."

From the hallway, Papa's head appeared, his eyes dancing with amusement. "From your reaction, I gather Helen has said yes?"

She nodded eagerly. "I have!"

Helen couldn't believe it. After four Seasons of hoping to find a husband, at last, she'd succeeded.

"In spite of the circumstances of how this engagement has come to be, it makes this old man so content to see both my daughter and future son happy." Papa reentered the room. "I just wish we knew who had started the viscous gossip."

"Papa, that is what I was pondering before Robert arrived."

Robert cleared his throat. "I believe I have an answer to your question. Without any shadow of a doubt, I can identify the culprit is none other than the disagreeable rogue Mr. Thomas Chapman."

"The scoundrel!" Mr. Davenport shouted, banging his fist on the table.

"I suspected as much." Helen gritted her teeth.

"Mr. Chapman is a distant cousin of mine and the godson of my late mother. She always harbored a soft spot for him, despite his knack for getting into trouble. After Mr. Chapman's father fell upon hard times, it was mutually decided that my sister would become his betrothed. Yet due to unforeseen circumstances, that never came to pass."

Robert swallowed hard.

"I tried to do right by my late family's wishes, and as a man of honor, I released half of my sister's fifty thousand pounds to him on the condition he was to assist his family. But as I have seen since time and time again since we were boys, he cares only for himself. Mr. Chapman burned through the twenty-five thousand pounds in the span of one year on drink, horseflesh, and cards. With my refusal to release any additional monies, Mr. Chapman blames me for 'depriving him of the life he deserves to live.'"

"The morning of the accident, the riderless horse I was chasing in Hyde Park belonged to our mutual foe. As he has in the past, he had imbibed in too much drink and fell off his horse, letting it run free. It was he who spotted us together."

Twenty-five thousand pounds, if used properly, was enough to last a person a lifetime. To hear Mr. Chapman spent that much in one year. Helen shivered. She had never been more grateful to Papa for his ability to see men as they truly were.

"Should you seek to question the veracity of my story, please speak to—"

"That will not be necessary." Papa held up his hand. "The better question now is how will we handle Mr. Chapman?"

"I have long been purchasing my wayward cousin's debts." Robert's brow furrowed. "He and I are long overdue to have a tête-à-tête. I intend to make him aware that this is his final warning. Unless his behavior undergoes an about face, I will have him sent to debtor's prison. He has harmed me, and now Miss Davenport, for the final time."

Helen thought Robert looked as she might picture the sea god Poseidon, ready to punish Odysseus for blinding his Cyclopes son in Homer's *Odyssey*. She would not wish to make an enemy of her future husband.

Epilogue

"My daughter is getting married."

Helen blinked back her tears whilst watching her father dry his own eyes. "Papa, we cannot start this again," she cried, her voice low.

"There will be no tears today. Only happiness," Aunt Sarah said.

"Your aunt is right." Papa held Helen's right hand. "Today is a day to celebrate a melding of two minds and kindred spirits." He sniffed.

Helen dabbed her cheek lightly.

Uncle William burst in just then. "The archbishop has arrived."

Five minutes later, Helen stood at the door to the church with her father, her arm hooked around his. In her hands was the most beautiful bouquet—a mix of orange blossoms, white roses, and hyacinths. Her bridal gown was an exquisite light green, adorned in hundreds of tiny pearls and trimmed with gold and ivory embroidery. On her neck, she wore a coral collared necklace, the same one her mother had worn on her wedding day.

Her father smiled down at her. "Are you ready?"

She let out a shaky exhale. "As ready as I'll ever be."

The pipe organ began to play.

Papa chuckled. "It's time to hand you over to His Grace." He kissed her on the cheek.

She inhaled deeply as the doors to the church opened, revealing a congregation of well-wishers and family. Her eyes, however, went straight to the man at the end of the aisle.

Her stomach somersaulted as Robert smiled wider than she had ever seen. His eyes brimmed with so much hope and admiration. His grey pinstriped waistcoat, blue tailcoat, and trousers accentuated his turquoise eyes. She took all of him in, still having a difficult time believing this was her wedding.

Following the directions of the clergyman, her father handed her over to her soon-to-be husband, kissing her forehead once more. Robert squeezed her hand. They faced the archbishop, and before Helen could process all that was happening, the couple exchanged rings, and shortly thereafter, was pronounced husband and wife.

Her heart pounded as they drew closer.

"You are so beautiful," Robert whispered, low enough so only she could hear it.

Her lips parted as they moved into one another. Robert wrapped his arms around her, and they kissed. To Helen, it was as if a butterfly had landed on her arm and its delicate wings were fluttering softly. Internally, new sensations and emotions stirred.

So, this is love.

She would never forget the bliss that filled her as they walked up the aisle together, or the happy smiles her father, Uncle William, and Aunt Sarah beamed at her.

Outside the church, a carriage awaited them. As Helen was handed up by a footman in gold-and-red livery, she smoothed out her skirt, before sitting down upon a sharp object. She lifted the thin rug to investigate the source of the discomfort. To her utter surprise, a brown-paper-wrapped parcel lay hidden in wait.

The carriage rocked as Robert climbed inside. The door was shut and steps lifted. "Walk on." He tapped on the roof. "Helen, what do you have there?"

She paid him no mind as she removed her gloves and quickly untied the paper. Carefully peeling it back, gold lettering revealed the title: *The Odyssey.* She rubbed the rim of the book.

"I discovered its sister volume the first afternoon call that you paid me. I'd always wondered whether you intended to intentionally hide the book or if you had dropped it by accident."

Robert studied the ceiling.

"Husband?"

"That's a new nickname. I shall note that I am 'husband' when you are cross with me."

She frowned. He laughed.

"Robert?" Helen tried again.

He crossed his arms and sighed. "When I discovered you already held a fine copy of *The Iliad* in your possession, I debated on what I should do. And so I decided to leave the book behind to have you make the decision for me. As I have come to learn, women know best."

"I can't fault you for that." Helen smiled broadly. "This set will be the only copies of Homer's writings I own in English."

Rising in the carriage, she wobbled on unsteady legs and sat beside her husband. "I owe you a thank you," she said.

She nuzzled her nose against his and kissed him the first of many times en route to the wedding breakfast. For the entire journey from the church to Curzon Street, Helen would only remember the sound of reverberating laughter, the scratchiness of Robert's cheeks rubbing against her own, and the endless strong, muscular embrace of her husband's arms wrapped around her body.

Dear Reader

Thank you for taking the time to read "The Mysterious Mr. Marcellus."

If you enjoyed this book, please take a moment to leave a review on Amazon, Goodreads, Bookbub, or whatever platform you may have discovered this book on. It helps Tomi connect with readers like you!

Love her books? Become a part of her treasured community here.

Stay connected with Tomi by scanning QR code, or by visiting her official website.

Https://TomiTabb.com

98

Acknowledgments

Thank you so much to my amazing team, Joanne, Kaylee, and Ranee, none of this would be possible without you three ladies. To my beta readers and especially Louise, thank you for your input and advice. You continually make each story stronger. Lastly to my readers, thank you for your positive feedback and encouragement. Two years ago, I never would have thought I'd have the courage to pen a Regency story, and yet, here we are.

About the Author

Tomi's publishing journey began in 2020 with the release of her debut novel, *Dancing With a Royal*.  Although she's always loved writing fictional stories, Tomi's background is in academic writing. She holds an MA degree in History and is currently pursuing her doctorate degree in the same subject.

In her rare free time, Tomi enjoys figure skating and hunting for new pumpkin flavored foods to try. It's one of the many reasons fall is her favorite season.

Tomi is a California native where she resides with her family and one very spoiled cat.

Website: TomiTabb.com

Also by Tomi Tabb

The Unexpected Royals

-Dancing With a Royal

-Jiving With a Royal

-Designing for a Royal

-More Than a Passing Shot

Friends of the Unexpected Royals

-Designs on Love

-Engineering Love

Novellas Related to the Unexpected Royals Series

-Pointe Shoes and Sugar Plums

-A Game of Small Victories

The Skaters of Sequoia Valley

-The Rules of the Rink

-The Sloth Zone

The Royals of Isola Nostrum

-The Great Austen Adventure

-For the Love of Dinosaurs

Historical Romance

-The Mysterious Mr. Marcellus